FOR ANDREW AND ADRIAN
AND 'THE COUSINS'

IN MEMORY OF AUNTIE LILIAN, WHOSE
UNTOLD STORY SPARKED THIS ONE.

'THE TIGER SKIN RUG IS SUCH A CHARMING
STORY, FULL OF MAGIC, HOPE AND
FRIENDSHIP. IT WILL FLY (LIKE A TIGER)
OFF THE SHELVES!'

MELVIN BURGESS

'A VIVID AND WARM-HEARTED TALE WHERE
THE FAMILIAR MEETS THE MAGICAL.
FROM A SCOTTISH VILLAGE TO AN INDIAN
MOUNTAIN, FROM THE BACK STREETS OF
LONDON TO THE PALACES AND SEWERS OF
MUMBAI, JOAN HAIG EXPLORES THE POWER
OF LEGENDS AND STORIES, FAMILIES AND
FORGIVENESS. A NEW VOICE YOU WILL
WANT TO HEAR MORE OF!'

JOAN LENNON

TIGER SKIN RUG

JOAN HAIG

pokey
hat

First published in 2020 by Pokey Hat

Pokey Hat is an imprint of Cranachan Publishing Limited

Copyright © Joan Haig 2020

The moral right of Joan Haig to be identified as the author of this work has been asserted by her in accordance with the Copyright, Designs and Patents Act, 1988.

ISBN: 978-1-911279-64-8

eISBN: 978-1-911279-65-5

Interior Illustrations © Marian Brown

Butterflies © Bloomella

Front Cover Illustration: © Purple Sky Design

Back Cover Illustration (London) © Krol / Denis Krasavchikov

www.cranachanpublishing.co.uk

@cranachanbooks

cranachan

'BEAUTIFULLY WRITTEN; SHIMMERS WITH MAGIC. BE TRANSPORTED ON A THRILLING ADVENTURE TO THE VIVIDLY EVOKED BACKSTREETS AND PALACES OF INDIA.'

LINDSAY LITTLESON

'A BEAUTIFULLY WRITTEN TALE OF MAGIC AND ADVENTURE, WITH HIGHLY RELATABLE CHARACTERS WHOSE DIVERSE CULTURES ARE SKILFULLY WOVEN TOGETHER IN A WONDERFULLY IMAGINATIVE PLOT.'

VICTORIA WILLIAMSON

'SPELLBINDING. THRILLING. HEARTWARMING. I DEVOURED IT IN ONE GULP.'

JENNI SPANGLER

A NEW HOUSE

My cricket coach said I was tall for my age, but the first time I stood in front of our new house, I felt as small as a wicket stump. If I'd known then what was inside the house, I would have felt even smaller. As it was, a wicket stump was miserable enough.

We'd just arrived in Scotland, tumbling out of the big red car after sixteen sweaty hours on aeroplanes all the way from India. Me—Lal Patel—my little brother Dilip, Mum and my grandmother, Naniji.

My father had picked us up from the airport. He looked paler than normal, but he was the same burly Baba, bouncing like a rubber ball. He'd gone ahead of us to sort things out, like buying a big red car and finding a house to live in.

"I've found the perfect place," he announced as he buckled his seatbelt. "First class."

I was sure it would be one of the slick city apartments

that Mum had spent hours and hours admiring on property websites. But as we drove from the airport, roads getting narrower and quieter, Baba broke the news. The house wasn't an apartment, and it wasn't in the city. "Don't worry," he said, "you'll love it—it's a bungalow in a nice, little town."

Nobody spoke. Not an apartment? Not in the city? Naniji rolled her eyes. It was no secret that in Naniji's opinion, Baba was a buffoon. The marriage wasn't a good match, she always complained; Mum was better than him in every way. I cringed—Naniji didn't think Baba could be trusted to choose which movie to watch on a Friday night and now he'd chosen the wrong place to live.

"And guess what?" he blundered on. "There's a whole acre of garden, and the house comes fully furnished."

"An acre?" shrieked Mum, whose idea of gardening was growing cress in cotton wool. "Fully furnished?"

"Yes!" Baba punched the steering wheel. "The house belonged to an elderly spinster who died without anyone to give things to. So, everything inside was included in the sale. It's a bargain!"

Naniji groaned. Undeterred, Baba grinned round to me and Dilip.

"And there are some superior items in the house, my boys, very superior indeed. It's like a museum."

I smiled weakly as if agreeing that, on some planet,

a museum was the perfect place to live in. Leaning my forehead on the cold car window, I watched raindrops form deltas on the glass. Outside, hundreds of Christmas trees tapered off to bare, purple hills. A church steeple appeared up ahead and soon we were chugging through the main street of the town. Baba steered us from its old-fashioned shops and touristy tearooms and turned into a leafy avenue. And there it was, the 'perfect place'. The big red car crunched up the drive to where I now stood, small as a wicket stump.

Naniji let out a cackle of unexpected glee. The bungalow wasn't an ordinary bungalow. It was huge and looming, with a deep verandah wrapped around its side like old houses in India, and a towering front door. The name 'Greystanes' was etched onto a pillar and a date— 1836—chiselled into the stone above. Baba brought out a ring of chunky keys, unlocked the door and waved us all inside.

Before anyone else had a chance, Mum raced in. She ran about the place, her arms flailing. The more she saw, the more she liked, and the more she liked, the more she shouted to Naniji.

"Look at the size of this room!"

"Have you seen the roll-top bath?"

Naniji went dashing after her, the scarf of her *salwaar kameez* flapping bright colours as she streaked from room to room. Baba traipsed in and out with suitcases, tripping over Dilip as he marched around pretending to be a storm-trooper.

My feet didn't march. They were stuck like gum to the hallway floor. I looked around me. A glass-domed ceiling threw dusty light onto fussy, flowery walls. Baba ruffled my hair.

"Come on in, my boy, welcome home!"

But it wasn't home.

Home was India, lush and green, in a modern housing compound with polished tiled floors and the top of a mango tree scratching the balcony. Home was my best friend, Ajay, and cricket fields and weekly trips to shiny shopping plazas. Home was NOT this big, old house in Scotland.

A brass plaque on a door to my right read, 'Drawing Room'. I imagined it stuffed with pencils and felt-tip pens. I wanted to find out what was inside, so I unstuck my feet, stepped closer and put my hand on the doorknob. *Click.*

Icy air licked up my shins. The room was dim, curtains drawn. Fumbling for a light switch, I heard the babble of everyone else coming up behind me.

"Lal!" they called, and, "Ooh, the 'Drawing Room'..." Mum said as they all bustled forwards and pushed me in. The babbling stopped. The room was cold and murky; a sour smell of old age and rotten flowers pinched our noses. And then I saw it, right in the middle of the room and staring across the darkness—a tiger.

It was a dead tiger, of course. Its skin was flat on the floor, dull and covered in cracks and scabs of dust. Its hideous head was propped up on its chin, big jowls set in a snarl. Its clouded glass eyes looked wrong. The rug looked wrong. The whole house and town and country were wrong, wrong, wrong.

Naniji squeezed my shoulder.

"Let's have some daylight," she said, sidestepping around the rug to tug at the curtains. A flutter of silvery house moths caught a sunbeam. Naniji opened the tall glass door and Dilip budged past me, out into the green morning. I shrank back to the hallway.

I didn't imagine I'd see anything creepier than a stuffed tiger head that day, but I was mistaken. That afternoon, Mum and Baba went out shopping. Dilip was playing around the place and Naniji was hanging things up—strings of lucky beads, a picture of the Hindu god *Ganesh*.

I hauled a suitcase to the bedroom. The walls were sunflower yellow. Two singles were made up, side by side. I lifted my case onto one and the mattress sagged. I sat next to it; I didn't feel like unpacking. What was it Baba had said? *Some very superior items in the house, very superior indeed.* Yes, I thought darkly, like dead tigers.

I wondered what Ajay would be up to now. Kitting up for cricket, probably. This was the first year I wouldn't be round at his house to binge on televised test matches and big bowls of popcorn…

Suddenly, I felt horribly alone. I went to find the others. Dilip and Naniji were in the kitchen, emptying cupboards.

"Have you been exploring?" Naniji asked.

"Not really," I shrugged.

"You should explore. Get to know the place." Naniji held up a dish cloth. "Or would you rather help me clean crockery?"

I turned on my heel and left the kitchen. I ran my fingers along a velvet settee in the study, admired cobwebs in the bathroom, and peeked into an airy dining room. I ended up at the front of the house, in the big entrance hallway and back at the door to the Drawing Room. I didn't want to go in there, didn't want to see the ugly tiger rug again, but I couldn't help it. It felt like something was pulling me towards it and before I knew what I was doing I'd pushed on the door and stepped in.

There was a clock on the mantelpiece, its broken hands hanging limp at the 'VI'. A stuffed ferret gawked down at me. I glared back and walked over to an upright piano in the corner of the room. The ivory keys were cold and rang an eerie discord that lingered even after I'd stopped pressing down. Two painted chests had been stacked against the back of a leather armchair. I ran my finger through the dust on top of one, but I didn't dare open it to see what was inside. Instead, I read the titles of books in a glass-fronted bookcase, faded novels arranged in alphabetical order: Kipling, Lofting, Nesb—

BANG!

The door slammed shut, and I jumped.

"Just a draught," I said to myself, though it had given me a fright. The doors to the garden were still open from earlier, so I closed them. When I turned back round, a little TV caught my eye. It was plugged in not far from the fireplace and at the tail end of the tiger skin rug. I knelt in front of it and pushed the power button. Nothing happened. I reached over and fiddled with some of the wires. The wooden boards pressed hard against my knees like the wrong size of shin guards.

"Come on, switch on, old thing," I whispered. "Come to life." I pressed the button a second time and this time something began to flicker in the grainy screen. "Yes!" I leaned back to see.

The image was hard to make out. There wasn't any sound, not even the hiss of static. Just shadowy lines, snake-like, moving from side to side. I switched the TV off and back on again. A little blue light twinkled and disappeared. Broken, I thought, and switched it off. But the picture in the screen didn't go away. The slithering thing was still there.

I squinted closer and froze.

The image wasn't coming from the television. It wasn't a broadcast. It was a reflection. Behind me, something was moving. Something on the floor behind me. And it kept on moving, getting closer—slithering, writhing, swelling. My shoulders pinched upwards, I took a deep breath, and I turned my head from the screen to see what was there.

Nothing. There was nothing there. That is, except the tiger skin rug, rigid and still. I darted my eyes back to the TV screen. Nothing there either, just a dusty reflection of myself.

This place was creepy. I got up and tiptoed to the nearest door—the one to the garden. I looked back at the space where something had moved—to where the rug lay. I got out and closed the door, making sure it was shut fast. And then I sprinted, faster than any home run I've ever made, running and running until I got to the other side of the house and could see, through the kitchen window, Dilip and Naniji hanging up garlands of plastic flowers.

"Lal, you look like you've seen a ghost!" Naniji said when I flew in. I opened my mouth to reply but no words came out. I rushed to her, breathing in the scent of safety and her fruity new perfume from Duty Free. Just then, Mum clattered through the other door, arms full of curious packets and tins from the grocery store, and a takeaway meal.

"Help me with these, will you, Lal?"

"What do you think of the house, boys?" Baba asked later on as we sat at the kitchen table eating dinner.

"I like it," said Dilip. "Except for the freaky tiger. Why did the old lady have that?"

I swallowed my mouthful of garlic bread and looked at Baba.

"Ah, yes," Baba said. "Well, the old lady, Miss Will was her name—"

"It's not to our taste," Naniji cut in firmly in Hindi, "but some people enjoy that sort of thing. Like eating chicken," and Naniji (a strict vegetarian) frowned pointedly at Baba who was now tucking merrily into a drumstick.

That first night in Greystanes, I lay awake for ages. It wasn't jet-lag or the new-out-of-the-packet sheets, or even Dilip's snoring. It was the tiger skin rug.

At first, it had made me feel sort of sad, like that famous picture Ajay showed me once—a cartoon from the olden days of the Raj when India was part of the vast British empire. It was a cartoon of a 'British' lion attacking and defeating an Indian tiger. At first, the rug had made me feel like that: defeated. But now, other feelings had crept in and taken over. Naniji had been joking when she said I'd looked like I'd seen a ghost, but it wasn't funny.

In fact, it was deadly serious. Greystanes was a haunted house.

2

A TRICK OF THE LIGHT

"Be careful!" I shouted at Dilip, who was teetering on a high wall. He always did crazy things like that. We were visiting a castle. Another one. The Patel family's third full day in Scotland and our third castle visit.

"I can see the moat!" Dilip yelled. I picked my way up the mound, clutching rocks and tufts of grass. The wall was built into the slope and when I stepped out onto it, my knees went all giddy. Baba jogged over, offering a hand. I took it and, when I was steady, I straightened right up and peered over to the other side. A lawn slanted down to a turret and a brown crescent of water.

They all looked the same, castles. Every time we reached one in our big red car, Dilip complained it wasn't like he'd imagined. It wasn't like I imagined either. Not a king, queen or knight in sight. Most of the time, there was barely any castle in sight either—just broken-down walls, sometimes even rubble. Grey stones and grey skies—nothing like India's rich greens and gleaming golds.

It started to drizzle. It drizzled a lot that first week. Drizzle (which was *not* like tropical rain) was as annoying as a swarm of mosquitoes—or worse, Scottish midges. Dilip drizzled tears at bedtime—never a downpour, never for long. There was a pile of American comic books in our room. We'd prop up in bed on plump feather pillows and I would read aloud how cartoon heroes with superpowers fought off villains. We'd seen one or two of the movies and played some computer games, but the comics were different: the drawings were old-fashioned and the pages were soft like cloth. In the mornings, when I woke up, Dilip would be curled up at my feet. I tried to make him laugh. "Greystanes," I'd say. "Like *grey stains*".

"I'm going to make a fire in the Drawing Room on Saturdays," Mum announced at the end of the week, "to keep out the damp."

I hadn't been in the Drawing Room since seeing the spooky reflection in the television—and I wasn't about to start hanging out in there. So, on that first Saturday, as soon as the logs were crackling, I went back to bed. Mum and Naniji were playing cards, Baba was reading his newspaper and Dilip was curled up on the tiger skin rug. From then on, if I couldn't find Dilip anywhere else, as sure as a cricket strike, he'd be sitting next to the tiger's head.

I was worried about him being in that room so much, but before I got a chance to warn him about the ghost, a second strange thing happened.

Mr. Stirling, the tall bald man from next door, had popped over with a box of eggs from his own chickens and Mum had invited him to stay for tea. She brewed up deep-tan *chai* and set a small cup in front of him, a filmy skin of milk floating on top.

I watched Mr. Stirling struggle to swallow it. And I watched Naniji nod and smile and form opinions, even though I knew she would barely catch a word of what was being said.

"Wonderful house," Mr. Stirling smiled. "Miss Will didn't invite folks in, not after she fell ill."

"Fell ill?" asked Mum.

"Yes," Mr. Stirling shook his head. "She lost her mind, I'm afraid. Poor woman."

Mr. Stirling and Mum chatted for ages. After a while, I slipped out to the bedroom and settled on my bed, balancing a stack of old stamp albums on my knees. Foreign drums, battleships, famous people's heads…

Suddenly, the door punched open and Dilip flew in.

He looked a bit crazy—scared and excited at the same time.

"What? What is it, Dilip?"

"The tiger. The tiger, come and see, come and see the tiger!"

I swung round and heard the albums thud to the floor. I didn't pick them up but chased after Dilip, who was already halfway down the corridor. I followed him through to the hallway and into the Drawing Room.

"Oh," Dilip sounded flat. "It's stopped."

"What's stopped? What happened?" But as Dilip crouched down, eyeballing the rug, I knew.

"Look!"

At first, I didn't see anything at all. Then spokes of dusty light fell through the tall glass doors and streaked across the tiger skin, and I swear the stripes rippled slightly, that its limp limbs twitched. It was dim in the room, but there it was again, a muscular movement from inside the rug. The bands on the tiger's tail began to slither, like the reflection on the old television, but real this time. Prickles came over my whole body. And then a rain cloud crossed the sun and the light raced away.

"Did you see it?" Dilip's eyes were wide.

"It's just a trick of the light," I said. The prickles had gone but my heart was beating on the outside of my chest. "I'm getting out of here. Come on, Dilip, come with me."

"No, Lal, wait, you won't believe what happened. The tiger rug, it started to move—"

"I've seen it before; I saw it first! Play in a different room, it's weird in here."

"But Lal—"

"Stop it, Dilip! It's creeping me out. Don't play in the Drawing Room any more."

From the hallway we heard a scuffle—Mr. Stirling was leaving. I put my finger up to my lips: the last thing I wanted was Mum asking questions. As soon as the front door clunked shut, I darted, my cheeks burning, back to the bedroom.

I sat back on the bed with the albums, but the stamps swam into a blurry puddle of colours on the page. What was in that room? Why had I blocked out what Dilip had been trying to say? Again, I knew the answer—Dilip had seen some sort of ghost, too. Maybe crazy old Miss Will was haunting the place, playing tricks with the old rug?

Suddenly, it was like a lightbulb pinged on over my head. I had the best idea. If Greystanes was already 'occupied', so to speak, then we couldn't possibly live here. Mum would freak out and Naniji would curse her lucky beads (and probably curse Baba). We'd all have to pack up and go back to India. It was obvious that the place already had a ghostly tenant.

All I had to do was prove it.

3

THROUGH THE WINDOW

Dilip didn't talk about the rug for the rest of the day or the following morning, and I didn't ask. The next afternoon, since the sun was shining, we went out into the sparkling garden.

"Cooee!"

I looked up at a fat wood pigeon, perched halfway up an evergreen. I frowned. Pigeons' calls were deeper, reedier.

"Cooee!"

It wasn't a bird. Further up the tree, almost at the top and half-hidden by a spikey canopy, was a freckly, frizzy-haired girl.

"Hello?" I called up to her, and she came crashing down the branches, scaring off the wood pigeon and jumping to land flat on her hands and feet. Standing up, broad-shouldered and boyish, she looked about my age.

"I'm Jenny," she said. "I live on the other side of Mr.

Stirling. Welcome to the neighbourhood. I saw you arrive ages ago, but you haven't been out to play yet."

"It's been raining," I replied.

"Raining? It's Scotland! A wee drop of rain never hurt anyone," and her words were like quavers and minims, singing up and down. "What's your name?"

"Lal," I said. "And this is Dilip."

Jenny scrunched up her freckly face then shrugged.

"Miss Will used to let me play here. Hope I still can? My hideout was Treehouse Corner, but I guess that'll be your base now. Anyway, my favourite bit's the Hidden Garden," and she pointed to a high hedge. "Want me to show you?" and she did cartwheels across the lawn. Dilip chased after her. I looked at them for a minute and then ran after them, sodden moss springing under my sandals.

Jenny led us to an opening in the hedge, hidden by bramble bushes and weeds that curled up like Indian vine snakes. Beyond it was a garden grown wild. Big, raised beds were overrun with plants of all shapes and shades. The pathway was half buried by long grass and speckled with tiny yellow and blue flowers. Jenny had Dilip by the hand, bossing him around.

"Gooseberries," she pointed as she talked, "blackcurrants, raspberries. Over there used to be the vegetables—you can still find onions. Let's pick some for your mum…" And she didn't stop talking as she yanked out withered little bulbs from the messy mass of green.

"Come and taste this, Lal!" Dilip called.

"It's wild spinach," Jenny said, holding out a green, frilly leaf. As I stepped to take it, I tripped on a matted clump of vines and Jenny shouted right at my face, "Stupid goose!"

Dilip giggled and I glared.

"What?" asked Jenny. "That's what it's called, that weed. Goosegrass. Though some people in Scotland call it sticky willy," she added, making Dilip wheeze.

"We get spinach at home in India, you know," I said, tears pricking the corners of my eyes. Though when I bit into the leaf, it was bitter and didn't taste like any spinach I'd ever known.

A flagstone path led to a cobbled circle in the centre of the Hidden Garden. Jenny hop-scotched along it; she was jabbering again.

From across the lawn, Mum called, "Lassi! Lassi!"

Jenny jumped.

"She's calling *me*! Why is she calling me? Did I do something? I'm the only lassie—why's she calling me?"

"Not a Scottish lassie," Dilip laughed. "*Lassi* in India is a yoghurt drink." Jenny threw back her head of wild, wiry hair and squealed. I smiled, sort of wishing I'd laughed like that when I'd tripped up.

We walked to the verandah. On an upturned crate, Mum had set out a glass jug and three stainless steel cups. Jenny handed her the onions.

"You must be Jenny," Mum smiled as she poured us each a generous helping of the thick milk drink. "Mr. Stirling has told me all about you." Jenny pinked, and Mum smiled. "Don't worry," she said as she turned to leave, "it was all nice things."

My lassi filled me with happiness—cardamom, brown sugar and Indian sea-sides; tangy tastes of things I missed, the sweets and sours of home. Jenny liked her milkshake, gulped it down: maybe she was OK, after all.

Over the rim of my cup, I watched her swing round the wrought-iron pillar, sticking out her leg and poking her feet right towards me. It was different here. People walked right into the house without taking off their shoes, sat down pointing their dirty soles right at you. People in India never did that—it was unclean and rude. Jenny's feet were tough, but her toenails, peeking out of her sandals, were purple with chipped varnish.

We sat, me and Jenny, tossing stones from the pathway onto the lawn, even though I knew Mum wouldn't like it. Jenny didn't seem to care. She'd gone quiet. Eventually, she stood up.

"I'd like to see inside Greystanes some time."

"Oh," I nodded. "OK."

"Miss Will let me play in the garden, but she never let *anyone* in the house. Even Mr. Stirling couldn't get past that front door. It was like there was a secret inside." Jenny paused. "Is there?"

I wasn't sure what to say, so instead I picked up a long twig and started stripping its bark. There *was* a secret in Greystanes. I wanted to tell this funny girl about the dead tiger and how the light in the Drawing Room made it look like muscles moved inside it. But I didn't say anything—if it was a secret, it was Dilip's secret, too.

The twig was in bits. Where was Dilip, anyway?

"Promise you'll show me?" Jenny asked, and as soon as I nodded, she skipped away.

I watched as she went. *Had* Miss Will been hiding the tiger skin rug? How much had she known about it? Maybe it was illegal… The year before, in school, Ajay and I had done a project on poaching. In the olden days, people wanted tiger skins as hunting trophies and rugs. These days it was their whiskers and bones for medicines and wine. Some people thought tiger bone wine gave them super powers and chest hair, my teacher had said. I shuddered. Wine from tiger bones sounded even more revolting than wine from squashed grapes.

A raven croaked, brought me back to where I was, sitting on the verandah getting cold. I knew where

Dilip would be: in the Drawing Room next to the rug. I stepped to the side of the tall window to spy on him. What did he do in there?

Dilip had sidled up to the tiger's ear and started talking. At first it was in whispers and then he became all animated, throwing his arms about. The sun was dazzling; I cupped my hands to my eyes and against the glass to see into the room. Whatever it was I thought I was going to see, it wasn't this.

Dilip kept on waving his arms and whispering to the tiger. Slowly, his words turned into white wisps, curling and whirling around the Drawing Room. Dilip was like a sorcerer or a mad conductor whipping up a distant music. Suddenly, he stopped and leaned backwards on his arms and scuttled sideways like a crab, away from the rug.

I pressed in closer to the glass. The wisps danced across the tiger's skin. It was clear this time: this was no trick of the light.

Something—what was it?—was rippling across the tiger skin, rippling up from underneath it. The ripples were growing. Tendons stretched and pulled against the tiger's fur. Its tail lengthened, filling out and rising, a banded torso taking shape. In no time at all, its shoulders had curved and its legs were pushing its bulk solidly upwards. It was coming to life. The tiger skin rug was coming to life.

I grabbed the door handle and jerked it down, but it was locked from the inside. I yelled and threw myself against the glass. Hammering at the handle, I looked up to see the beast twisting around towards Dilip. I sprinted, frantic, tripping at the green gate, falling on the gravel. Scrambling up, I felt the heat of grazed palms but didn't look down, kept going, flew in through the huge door and bolted across the hallway.

"Dilip!" But when I got to him, my voice, and my courage, fell away.

"Dilip?"

4

THE TIGER AND THE RUG

The tiger was so big it was like the room shrank. It shifted from one side to the other on hefty paws. I pressed out my hand to Dilip, but couldn't take my eyes off the tiger. It turned and looked straight back at me. Its eyes, instead of glued-in glass, were honey-golden and blinking with life. I was so fixed on the tiger, I didn't notice until hearing the *thud* and *click* that Dilip had crept to the door and shut us in. Actually *shut us in* with the tiger.

"Dilip?"

"It's OK, Lal. It's not what you think."

I didn't know what I thought.

"He's my friend. He won't hurt you." Dilip's thin arm was at the tiger's mane, which was thick and glossy and gave the cat a kingly look. Its jaw dropped in a yawn, revealing a rack of glinting teeth. My jaw dropped, too—at seeing all those canines and carnassials, tools for seizing and shearing flesh. There were more teeth than I remembered. There was more of the whole thing than I imagined. Dilip was stroking it like it was the neighbourhood moggy.

"Come closer, Lal," Dilip said in a soft voice. I considered the invitation. The tiger had a faint, warm glow—what Naniji would call an aura—wavering around it. It didn't seem angry. Or hungry. But what did I know about that? "Don't touch him," said Dilip. "Just hold out your hand. Keep it still, let him come to you. Don't scare the tiger."

Scare the *tiger*? I did what I was told. Well, mostly—I held out my hand, but I couldn't stop it quaking. Before I knew what was happening, the tiger had leaned forwards and was pressing its forehead against my palm. Like a current of electricity zipping between two poles, something wild and raw connected us. Something new and ancient, impossible and yet true. Despite everything, I felt suddenly calm. I breathed out.

"See?" said Dilip, pulling me to sitting.

The tiger spiralled down with a *humph*. Its nostrils flared. Its nose was moth-shaped, I noticed. Dilip looked so little and the tiger so... so real. We sat a while not speaking as everything I knew about anything scrambled and re-coded.

"How did it happen?" I asked. "How long have you known?" And Dilip said it had all started when he needed somewhere to be alone, when he was missing

24

India. Nobody came into the Drawing Room much because nobody liked seeing the rug. But he didn't think it was so bad, so he escaped here every so often.

"Then one day I started telling it stuff," he shrugged. "And I saw that when I whispered, the tiger skin looked all wavy."

We both looked at the tiger.

"Lal, there's magic, when I whisper. And the more I whisper, the more the magic makes the tiger… come alive."

I frowned. I knew there was no such thing as magic (I was nearly twelve, after all). Magic was made-up, in stories. And yet, here we were… I touched the tawny fur of the tiger's neck.

"Weren't you frightened?" I asked, thinking of the reflection in the TV that first day.

"A bit. Mostly that you wouldn't believe me. I tried to tell you."

"I know."

"There's something else, Lal."

"What? What is it?"

What else could there possibly be? Dilip took a deep breath.

"The tiger talks back to me." At this, the tiger gave a short, snarly yawn and I glimpsed its other teeth, embedded in purple gums and yellowed like the ivory piano keys. When it was a rug, I'd tried not to look at the tiger's mouth, especially not at its fake, varnished tongue. Now I couldn't stop looking—especially at its tongue, salmon pink and licking with life. Its blonde chin juddered lightly in another yawn that finished with the hot, stale smell of tiger breath. Was it alive or dead? How could it talk?

"Lal? Dilip? Lal?"

Mum was calling us. We glanced at each other and jumped up. Dilip pulled me to the settee so that the tiger could slope back to the floor. It was clear that Dilip had done this lots of times before. Collapsing downwards, the tiger's aura vanished, its body disappeared, stripes faded. Feeling dizzy, I held onto the sofa and squeezed my eyes shut as the whole room seemed to shudder and fill with a terrifying emptiness.

It lasted only seconds, and when I opened my eyes again, I was dazzled by daylight. A raven was calling. And there it was, the tiger skin, nothing more than an old and dusty piece of taxidermy. Dilip had gone, leaving the Drawing Room door wide open.

Mum had called us because Dilip had to go out with Baba to buy new shoes. I was to stay home and help sort out the pantry. Just my luck—stuck sorting packets and jars when there was a magical tiger across the hallway.

I couldn't concentrate, was too desperate to know.

What if I were to whisper to the rug, would it come to life? Or was it only Dilip that could do the magic? My head was throbbing with questions. I knew how to score cricket, loved algebra and brain teasers, but this was different. I didn't have any answers. By accident, I poured black peppercorns into the rice tin and labelled the Thai green curry 'tiger curry'.

"Right," sighed Mum. "Go and find some fun. Go on, Lal—do something else." And I knew exactly what something else to do.

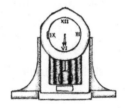

Back in the Drawing Room, I lowered myself next to the head of the tiger skin rug.

"Can you come alive?" I asked. My question was swallowed into a lengthy silence. "Please?" I added. "I just need to know if it's only Dilip that can, you know, wake you up, or..." I could sense the ferret, with its beaded eyes, laughing down at me. I tried to ignore it. Stroking the tiger's forehead, I remembered the electric feeling when the tiger had touched my palm. I ran my fingers across to its black-and-white ears and leaned in to whisper closer. Nothing happened.

It wasn't fair that little Dilip was the one that got to magic up the tiger. If only I'd whispered more that first day, maybe it would have come alive for me. I stood up, feeling a bit silly. Not too silly to turn and say, tiptoeing to the door, "I saw you first, didn't I? In the TV screen. It was you, wasn't it?"

The next day was the last before Mum and Baba started their jobs in the city and Dilip and I would get to stay all day with Naniji. Baba had planned a drive to an old estate house followed by a splash at the beach.

The estate house was grand and cold—much grander and colder than Greystanes. I tugged Dilip into one of its spiral stairwells.

"What do you mean, the tiger talks to you, Dilip?" I demanded. There was a soft echo in the stone chamber.

"It just speaks to me."

"How?"

"I don't know." Dilip wrinkled his nose.

"It says words?"

"I think it does, but not really out loud."

"Telepathy?"

"Maybe, yeah, sort of."

"But you talk out loud to it?"

"Yes, well, sometimes."

"So, what does it say?"

"It tells me not to worry," said Dilip, "and I think it needs help, Lal. It says it wants to be free." Dilip hopped down a step, and then down two.

"What does that mean? Free from what?"

But Dilip had jumped too far ahead and rounded a corner. The steps were steep—I held on to the rope banister on my way down and by the time I'd caught up with Dilip, so had the grown-ups. Mum and Naniji were gazing at a wall-sized tapestry and Baba lingered in front of a portrait of po-faced men in hunting gear. We all walked together towards the exit.

Fifteen. I was counting dead animals. There weren't only the usual antlers. *Twenty-two.* There were fox furs draped over armchairs, cow hide carpets on the floor, and exotic birds in bell jars. *Twenty-nine.* I wondered what they would say if they could come alive and talk. Could they? *Thirty-three.*

Baba ruffled my hair. "Let's get some lunch!"

Thirty-three dead animals.

Down at the seaside, we bought fish and chips in paper parcels from a van in the car park. We set out deckchairs near a big, white lighthouse. When the curry sauce Naniji had opted for with her chips turned out to be a thick spicy vinegar, she pulled a face that made us all laugh. We washed our food down with 'Scotland's National Drink,'

a sweet fizzy soda the colour of Halloween pumpkins.

As the shadow of the lighthouse fell across us, we scraped our chairs into the last patch of sunshine. Mum sat with Naniji, who hugged into her sari and woolly cardigan, their backs to the wind. Naniji scolded Baba when he came howling from the shoreline where he'd dared to dip knee high into the icy sea.

I raced Dilip up and down lines of dried seaweed, salt wind stinging our faces, crashing down to the sand feeling wild and free.

Wild and free. Like the tiger wanted to be. I dug with frozen fingers, as if there might be answers buried in the sand. A living tiger in a trap could be set free. But this was not a living tiger. And it was stuck in no ordinary trap.

5

PANCAKE STORIES

Mum and Baba were out of the house before Dilip and I were out of bed. Naniji let us stay late in our pyjamas playing computer games. Later, she brought to the verandah trays piled high with hot samosas, sticky jalebi twists and coconut cubes to scoff between our cricket innings. She kept score, but also kept nodding off on the wicker chair.

"Naniji," I coaxed, "why don't you go and lie down properly?"

She stirred, smiled, and shuffled away for an afternoon nap. As soon as she'd gone, I dropped my bat, Dilip dropped the ball, and we dashed to the Drawing Room.

I was skittish and jumpy, like a lone deer that strayed too far into tiger territory. I stood behind the armchair. Dilip, though, plonked himself right next to the tiger's big head. I watched as he began to whisper. His whispers took shape in the air by themselves, just like they'd done when I'd been peeping through the window. He was like a ventriloquist, his mouth hardly moving.

The stripes on the tiger shifted; Dilip slid backwards on the floor, licking his lips. Mine were oat-dry and I couldn't swallow. I could hardly breathe. Dilip's whispers were bringing the tiger to life. Its body was forming, turning itself round and round until it was real and whole and the room was filled with its hugeness once again. It shook itself out and stretched its paws forward.

Dilip clapped and lunged towards the big cat, giving it a hug. The air seemed to clear of his whispers. The tiger's eyes were deep circles of saffron yellow, amber and black. When it blinked at me, my heart soared. The tiger's stripes, unique as a fingerprint, streaked down from its back and to the insides of muscular legs. At the sides of its face, the white tufted mane looked brighter than before.

"Sit," said Dilip, patting the floor next to him; and the tiger sat, lowering itself weightily down.

"Cool! That is *so cool*," and I couldn't believe I was saying that out loud about Dilip. He hugged the tiger again. I took a step out from behind the chair. I so badly wanted to hug the tiger, too. As if reading my mind, it pushed its paw towards me, so I slid closer in and laid my hand on top of its soft fur. Its claws were retracted inside bristly looking knuckles. "Does it ever get angry or anything?" I asked.

"Sometimes," Dilip drew his knees up to his chin and hid half his face. "I played at hunting once." The tiger's ears bent backwards and it made a puckering sound as if gearing up to growl. "It's OK," Dilip patted it, "I'm not playing that again."

"Why? What happened?"

"It did that thing with its ears. Only they went really far back and it—" The tiger gave another not-quite-growl, curling in its claws and furrowing its brow, and then let out a short snarl "—it did that!"

We sat and talked and watched. The tiger put its nose in the air when it heard threatening sounds, like Mr. Stirling's lawnmower. It nodded and gave a small shake of the head when we talked about India.

It felt so easy, sitting with a tiger.

Suddenly, the tiger pawed at Dilip. Naniji was up from her nap and singing in the kitchen. For the next few days, when Naniji napped after lunch, we sat with the tiger in the Drawing Room. It didn't 'speak' exactly, except in a way Dilip could hear, but its movements were signs and they became predictable. It always heard Naniji stir before we did.

Naniji let Jenny lead us off around town for hours. Jenny showed us the river and two small streams called 'burns', where Dilip spent ages building dams and I learned how to skim pebbles, making flat ones bounce across the water surface like jet skis. We steered pedaloes at the park and kicked footballs about with other town kids. And Jenny told us little by little about how she'd come to live with Granny.

"My mum and dad died when I was three," Jenny announced one day as we stood barefoot on the river verge throwing sticks into the rapids. I squinted against the sun's glare, not knowing what to say. Luckily, Jenny kept talking. "We lived up north. But after they died, I came here to live with Granny. She sorted me out."

I'd waded out further and deeper into the freezing water and lost the feeling in my toes.

"Tell Jenny," Dilip said. "Tell her about the tiger."

"What tiger?" asked Jenny, and her ears pricked up just like one. I decided to start at the beginning. How we were homesick. How I'd thought Greystanes was haunted. And how, when Dilip whispered to the tiger skin rug, the tiger came to life. Jenny had stopped throwing sticks and was standing listening, believing every word. "I told you Miss Will had a secret!" she said. "I bet that was it, a magic tiger!" She kicked her foot into the water. Dilip jumped down and sat on a clump of earth and we all sank into our own thoughts.

"Come on," rallied Jenny after a while. "I'll take you to Granny. She'll sort you out. I mean, about missing home and all that."

We strapped on our shoes and squelched back across the town square and up the road to the avenue where we lived.

Granny's house was a bungalow too, but smaller and smelling of burnt toast. There was a table with a telephone on it, and an umbrella stand full of tennis rackets and a scuffed-up cricket bat.

"Come in, you lot! Come in!" Granny wasn't as old as I'd imagined. She had short, spiked-up brown hair and was wearing jeans and a worn-out man's shirt. "I was taking a tea break from gardening," she said, "so let's all have some pancakes."

We followed her into to the kitchen where there was a big stove with a heavy flat pan hanging above it. Granny reached to get the pan down.

"Now, sit down, everyone," she said. As she mixed flour, eggs and milk in a bowl, she began to talk. I thought she was talking to herself at first (the way Naniji did), but she was telling a story. Jenny said later that Granny always did that, told 'Pancake Stories'. This one was called 'Rashiecoats' and it was about a princess who was ordered to marry a horrible prince and live in a far-off place.

"The princess was having none of that. She dressed herself in rushes from the river, pretended to be poor and ran away. She set out on a long journey to find her true love." Granny's voice sang high and low, like Jenny's, and even though it was a love story, there were no kissing bits and we were on the edge of our seats at Rashiecoats' adventures.

On to the hot, flat pan went little circles of batter, which bubbled up into scrumptious little cakes. By the time Rashiecoats was living happily ever after, Granny had made a plateful of pancakes.

"Now, these are Scotch pancakes, boys," she said, showing us how to layer on top a thick blade of butter and coating of strawberry jam. "A bit different to the food in India, am I right?"

Jenny kicked me under the table.

"Lal and Dilip miss India, Granny."

"Ach, of course you do," she nodded. I looked at Dilip, whose cheeks were bulging. "Just you settle down and stop worrying about it. It takes time," she winked at Jenny.

"Everything's so different," I said, licking my fingers clean of jam.

Granny sighed and sat back. Her face was tanned and there were wrinkles—the kind you get from smiling—at the sides of her eyes.

"Difference isn't a bad thing," she said at last. "Quite the opposite. Think how dull life would be if everywhere and everyone were the same." She fiddled with her knife. "You'll make up your own mind where you belong. Not even your parents, only you, can decide that."

"Like Rashiecoats," Dilip piped up.

Not really, I thought.

"A wee bit, yes," Granny smiled.

36

I wasn't sure if it was the pancakes, the story-telling, or the things Granny had said, but Jenny had been right, I felt a whole lot better.

Later, back at Greystanes, I sat playing cards with Naniji in the kitchen. Dilip was in the Drawing Room with the tiger, so I tried to distract Naniji for as long as possible. Just as I heard the slamming doors of the big red car, Dilip appeared.

"The tiger's upset," he said, out of Naniji's earshot.

"What about? Were you playing hunting again?"

"No, I wasn't. I asked some questions. I asked if he was a secret. And where he came from. He started walking in circles." I pictured the tiger pacing like big cats in captivity, wild cats driven demented by being caged.

"What else? What did it tell you?"

"It told me it needs our help. It wants to tell us its story. Tomorrow afternoon, with Jenny."

Before I could ask him anything else, Mum and Baba burst in with flowers for Naniji and a thousand questions about our day, but all I could think of was tomorrow.

6

THE TIGER'S PROMISE

Dilip sat cross-legged next to the tiger rug. I was on the settee, which Naniji had reupholstered in clear plastic to keep the stains off.

"Naniji, please can you help light a fire before you take a nap?" Dilip asked. "We want to play in here with Jenny."

Naniji liked Jenny, and before she went for her nap, she got the fire going. I helped by stacking kindling into a pyramid shape around scrunched-up newspaper.

Jenny had been hovering outside. I opened the French doors for her and then locked them tight when she was in, drawing the curtains. Jenny, unusually, didn't say a word as she sat down next to Dilip. I switched on a reading lamp, tipped it down so the bulb shone low, and sat on the other side of her.

Dilip stroked the brow of the tiger's head, smoothing its fur upwards from its eyes. As he started to whisper, the shape of the tiger began to shift. The tiger was twisting now, twisting around and into life. It shook out its whiskers and gnawed and licked in between its claws. The tip of its tail tapped gently, up and down. Jenny had squirmed up so close I could smell her hair—a plastic, pink smell not like anything else about her, except maybe her purple toenails.

The tiger arranged itself like a sphinx and stared right at Jenny. Jenny stared back. Tigers don't usually like being stared at, but maybe Jenny wasn't much of a threat. She'd definitely lost her usual spark and was gripping my arm so tight it hurt.

The tiger closed its eyes. From nowhere and everywhere there came a low language, far away and old as the hills. It faded, but Dilip heard it still, I could tell.

"The tiger has a promise to keep," Dilip didn't look up as he spoke. The tiger's ears flicked and its neck tensed. Dilip dipped his head and raised his shoulders. This must be how they spoke to each other. Dilip put his hand on the tiger and his hand looked so small. The tiger squirmed and I wasn't sure we should be there at all. Maybe this whole thing was too dangerous—not the tiger itself, but the sorcery. Dilip's little hand stayed on the tiger and the tiger settled down. His whispers and his touch were like spells. Another long silence followed.

"The tiger was poached," Dilip said at last. "He was going to do something important. He was on the way to do something important when he was shot down dead."

I shivered and Jenny gasped. Obviously, it had been shot. We knew that—anyone could see there was a bullet hole in its pelt. And it wasn't exactly alive, being stretched out flat as a chapatti most of the time. But there was something shocking about it all the same, something unsettling about the word 'poached'.

"What was it was going to do?" I asked. "What was the important thing?" There was another long wait.

"A message. He was trying to give someone a message." Dilip looked up at me. "He promised to give someone a very important message but was shot before he could keep his promise."

"Who was the message for?" Jenny ventured.

"He doesn't know the name, he doesn't remember things like that." Dilip paused. "He can't rest until the promise is fulfilled, and he wants us to help him keep the promise."

I looked at the tiger, the firelight in its eyes. I felt sad, because the story was sad. But inside me, another kind of fire was burning. I got up and padded to the door. I opened it a crack, checking Naniji was still out of sight, and then carefully closed it.

"There's only one thing to do," I said, my voice growing bolder as I looked at the tiger. "We have to help."

Jenny squealed in agreement and suddenly we were all talking, plotting, laughing.

"Granny can help—she's full of good ideas!" Jenny said.

"That's a top plan!" agreed Dilip.

"I'm not so sure," I lowered my voice. "Involving adults could be risky."

"You're right, we can do this ourselves," Jenny squealed again. Dilip started hopping about the floor on all fours, kicking his legs up like a hare. Jenny clapped her hands. We were all talking and talking, didn't notice our voices rising or footsteps in the hallway or the opening of the Drawing Room door.

But it's difficult to take a tiger by surprise. A tiger's hairy ears swivel around and prick up at the slightest sound of danger. So, by the time the door was opening, the tiger had shrunk back flat. Dilip, spinning round and dizzy, stumbled straight into Naniji.

"Dilip, be careful!" she scolded in Hindi. Our eyes all darted to the tiger and we breathed out in relief at seeing it as a rug on the floor. "What noise!" continued Naniji. "I could hear you from the other side of the house. What are you playing?"

All at the same time, we shouted, "Wrestling!", "Spiderman!" and "Tiger Hunts!"

I wasn't always able to tell if Naniji was angry or not—grown-ups are a bit unpredictable, and not at all like tigers in that way. You know where you stand with a tiger. Naniji moved to the window and opened the curtains. "A game of superheroes wrestling tigers?" she said with a smile, pushing open the glass door. "Go out and play," and, in Hindi, "Tell Jenny it's nearly time she went home to her own grandmother."

We scuffed out. Dilip was the last to leave. He hovered at the door, looking at the rug. I reckoned he was thinking of his whispers. His whispers and how he could do magic. Jenny snatched at me and raced away.

"You're It!"

For the next few days, it proved impossible to get together and plan. For a start, Jenny and her Granny had visitors, so she couldn't come over. And, of all things, Mum decided to revamp the Drawing Room, so we couldn't even talk to the tiger. We carried out antlers, the ferret and stuffed owls, reading lamps and armchairs. Pictures were taken down, leaving faded rectangular marks on the dark green walls. Everything was packed in boxes for sending to a jumble sale. Everything except the old clock on the mantelpiece (which Mum had had fixed), and the tiger skin rug.

Passing the room, I saw Mum and Baba standing over the rug and I overheard them saying things like, "It really must go" and, "The sooner the better", so I dodged behind the door to eavesdrop.

"And this man said he'd pay a good price?" Mum was asking.

"Yes, yes, his offer was generous," Baba replied. "He said he'd been looking for a tiger skin rug like this one for some time."

My stomach flipped. Someone wanted to buy the rug. We had to stop them.

"He's Indian, did I say that?" Baba was saying. "And quite a character—long hair and dressed head-to-toe in black except for this silver snake embroidered on his leather jacket. Naniji would have a thing or two to say about him, I'm sure. I told him to come back, that I'd talk to you first."

If Mum and Baba sold the rug, what would happen to the tiger and its promise? Where would the tiger be taken by the man in the snake jacket? And, not only that, with the 'ghost' gone, how could I convince Mum and Baba to take us back home?

7

PLOTS AND PLANS

The Drawing Room was lighter without all the dark, fancy things weighing it down. I'd been sitting with the tiger skin rug for a while, thinking again about what Mum and Baba had said. I stroked the tiger's face. There was no way I could let them sell it. If the plan was to sell soon, we'd have to act sooner.

"We'll help you, we will," I whispered, and, did it? Did something stir? Only my imagination. I ran my palm down the back of the rug, from the tiger's neck to its bristly, stunted tail. The rug was tatty at the hind, and part of the backing had worn away. I lifted a corner to see what it was like on the other side, imagining sinewy leather. Instead, it was backed in satin.

A thick, loose thread was too tempting not to pull on, but it ripped more than I meant it to. Turning the corner up further to see how much I'd torn, I found, fixed on with a rusty staple, a faded label.

SOLD BY J. ECKS AUCTIONEERS, LONDON, SE1.

J. Ecks. London. I re-read the label and thought about what it meant. The rug must have been sold at auction in London. Whoever it was, J. Ecks could surely tell us where the tiger had come from. I dropped the corner of the rug and ran to tell the others.

I whistled Dilip down from the treehouse and we waved hurriedly to Mr. Stirling on the way to Jenny's. She was out washing Granny's car—she got pound coins for jobs like that.

"We've got to go to London," I said, and told them about Mum and Baba wanting to get rid of the rug and about the label and Ecks Auctioneers. Jenny put her bucket down. She nodded towards Mr. Stirling.

"He's got a whole collection of maps. I can ask to borrow some."

"Tops," I replied.

"And you have to find out more about Ecks," Jenny said. "And don't tell anyone. Nobody say anything to anyone else about any of this." Jenny crossed her heart with her index finger. "Swear on your life that you won't tell a soul."

Dilip crossed his heart and they both looked at me. Reluctantly, I pledged to die if the secret got out.

I hung back with Baba while the others walked to the park.

"Baba, can I please use the Internet?"

Baba was on the verandah, swinging on an old rocking chair.

"What for?"

"I wanted to search for someone," I replied vaguely, not wanting to say anything about J. Ecks Auctioneers. "I'm seeing if there are… any other Patels in Scotland…" I burbled.

Baba sprung up like a jack-in-the-box. His favourite pastime was searching for people's family trees online. Especially the family trees of Indians like us who had come to the UK.

"Any other Patels in Scotland? Any other Patels? Boy, there are hundreds! There are generations!" And he was looking at me wildly, whooping, "There are Patels all over the planet!"

I didn't care right now—it was Ecks I was after. (And was that even true? Patels everywhere? I hadn't seen a single Indian anywhere in our new town so far.) Baba whooped again. "Oh, this is exciting! So, let me tell you this, I'm building an online database, Lal—a *Hindus' Who's Who of Who's Here*."

I raised my eyebrows at Baba's tongue-twisting idea, and was glad Naniji wasn't here to cluck through her teeth at him.

"It's on the homepage—check it out! All prominent families in the UK. Names, addresses, everything! Go, yes, yes, go, if you're searching for someone, for Patels, then yes—let me know how you fare!" and Baba reached out for his customary ruffling of my hair. "Yes, you know what to do, right? You know the rules."

"Yes, Baba," I replied a little guiltily as Baba sat back, pleased as punch that his elder son was clearly as keen as he was on Indian genealogy.

Baba's laptop was sleek and new with a back-lit keyboard. I liked to pretend I was at a control centre, leader of a mission. This time it was sort of true. I was good at this stuff. On the homepage was the *Hindu Who's Who*. I ignored it and opened a new tab on the browser. My fingers zipped across the keys, typing into the search bar:

j ecks auctioneers london

I scrolled down the list but didn't see an official auctioneer's website. J. Ecks was in the London Gazette one year, and there were a couple of articles from magazines directing customers to Ecks's sales list, but none of the links were active. I clicked on 'Images' and a row of pictures of a shopfront appeared, and a few of antique objects. Again, none of the links worked.

But when I clicked on 'Maps', a box popped up with a little tear-shaped pin marking the auction house. There it was, J. Ecks Auctioneers, SE1. No website, that's all. (Lots of businesses didn't have one, right?) Zooming in, I figured out it was near Waterloo Station, wherever that was. Once we had Mr. Stirling's maps, we could easily find our way there. Satisfied, I closed the tabs, exited the browser, and logged off.

"Did you find what you needed?" Baba called. "What did you make of the database—superior, yes?"

"Yes, brilliant, thanks, Baba!" and I ducked away before more questions were fired.

As soon as Dilip was back from the park, I dragged him off to Treehouse Corner, where we whistled for Jenny to join us.

"I found it!" I couldn't keep the news in. "It's near Waterloo Station in London."

We talked about finding Ecks and the next steps in helping the tiger keep its promise. Jenny's giggles floated down and across to Mr. Stirling.

"I'll ask him for the maps," she said. "Come to my house in the morning and we can look at them and make a real plan."

"And I'll tell the tiger," Dilip nodded.

Just then, someone passed the other side of the treehouse, heavy footsteps grinding into the gravel.

"Who's that?" asked Jenny. I lifted my finger to my mouth. Through gaps in the wood I saw a dark figure ringing the doorbell. "Look!" she poked my arm. "It's the man with the snake jacket." And she was right. The man was dressed all in black, a glittering silver snake on his back. My heart sank. He must be here to buy the rug.

Mum answered the door.

"We have to stop him," I said, as he and Mum stood there talking. It was that time of evening when midges were out, biting at knees and elbows. "Come on," I urged when the others didn't move, "let's go." But the man had started to leave—without the rug. Jenny pulled me back into hiding. We tried to get a better look at him, but his head was dipped and hidden by his shoulder-length hair.

"This is way more urgent than I thought," I said when he was out of sight.

"Let's meet tomorrow, first thing," Jenny smiled reassuringly and clambered along a thick branch and scraped down the fence. Then Dilip and I climbed down the rickety ladder and raced back to the house to check on the tiger.

I was so distracted the next day that I smashed two plates helping Naniji wash up after breakfast. She tutted at me and then kissed me and her skin wrinkled into a smile. We were the same height now. She sent me and Dilip off to play.

When we knocked on Jenny's door, it was Granny that answered.

"Ah, the Patel boys! Come in, lads. Jenny's been cavorting about the place waiting for you since the cock crowed!"

I smiled at Granny's funny sayings. There had been a cockerel in India, in the neighbour's courtyard, which started crowing at 05:00hrs sharp every morning. Thankfully there wasn't one around here; that cockerel was *not* one of the things I was missing about India.

"What took you so long?" Jenny said bossily.

"We had to do the dishes first," I explained, slipping off my shoes.

"Did you hear that, Jenny?" Granny nodded approvingly. "These boys help their granny do morning dishes. Maybe you should try that. Tell you what, you can wash up after pancakes today."

Jenny threw spears at me with her eyes as she tugged Dilip across the hall to her bedroom.

Jenny's bedroom was small and untidy. A middle drawer was open, sleeves dangling out. Jenny followed my gaze to an old crisp packet, which she crinkled up and tossed towards an overfull waste-paper bin. She missed and shrugged.

"I got the maps," she said cheerfully, bouncing backwards onto her bed. "Can you read them? I can't. Though I've been to London before if that helps."

Next to a bent-open picture book on the floor was a tall tower of orange and grey folded maps. I reached across for one.

"We don't need maps," Dilip replied. "The tiger will get us there."

"What?" I looked up. "No, Dilip, no way. The tiger can't come with us." Besides, I'd already made a plan: study the maps, get train timetables, find out the cost of the fares, arrange somewhere to stay, *etcetera, etcetera*. The tiger was definitely not coming with us.

"The tiger is definitely coming with us," said Dilip. "It can retrace its path."

I knew from the mugging-up I'd done with Ajay that tigers have amazing place memory; if they've been somewhere before, they can often find their way back. But *this* tiger? A skin-and-ghost tiger? Taking us hundreds of miles to an unknown location?

"The tiger said to trust it," Dilip piped up, "and it asked me what I—what *we*—would like in return. I didn't know what Jenny wanted, but I told it we'd like to go home. Lal, the tiger promised that if we help it, it will take us home."

A glimmer of hope and longing crossed Dilip's face. We both wanted to go back to India so much. I imagined surprising Ajay and how good it would be to see him again.

Dilip looked smaller than usual, though his trust in the tiger was titanic. I sighed. How could the tiger take us home? It was impossible.

"I think we should look at the maps anyway," I said. "That way we'll have a plan if the tiger gets lost, or,"— worse—"if it gets found. We have to think ahead. Jenny, we'll need your pocket money, all of it." Jenny nodded.

"But the tiger, it *said*—!" shouted Dilip.

"The tiger can't keep such a wild promise, Dilip!"

Jenny jumped up. "Why not? You're being so bossy, Lal."

"I'm bossy? *I'm* bossy?" I yelled back.

"Yes, you. You're—"

There was a creak from the hallway and a voice glided in, "Everything all right there, Jenny?"

"Yes, Granny!" Jenny stepped towards me and lowered her voice. "Look, Lal, taking you home isn't exactly the first wild promise the tiger's made. It's keeping a promise right now. It can't rest until its promise is kept. Besides, you'll be *home* again—it's an extra reason to go," and she smiled at Dilip. "Going home was a brilliant thing to ask for in return."

I scowled at them both. "What else did the tiger say, Dilip?"

"It said to meet it in the Drawing Room tonight at 11 o'clock."

"Tonight?" yelped Jenny. "Wait, wait, what will I tell Granny? What will your parents say in the morning when you're not there? There'll be a search party. We can't run off in the middle of the night!"

I rolled my eyes, but Dilip didn't falter, the tiger had given him answers for everything. "Time will take care of itself," he said, and when he spoke, it was as though the tiger was speaking. The room became charged with its energy, like the words were charmed. *Time will take care of itself.*

"What does that mean?"

"And how will we know exactly where to go?" I pressed.

"The tiger will take us," Dilip said.

My irritation cracked through the magic. "Dilip! How on earth can the tiger know where to go? And how exactly are we going to get anywhere with a *tiger*?"

"That's what the *tiger said*," Dilip persisted.

From across the house Granny called out, "Pancakes!"

"Coming, Granny!" called Jenny. She turned to me. "So, what are we going to do? Are we going to meet at 11? Lal? Are we going to London?"

I sucked in a breath. What if the tiger *could* get us

there, and what if it really could take us home? It was magical, after all. And Dilip and Jenny didn't seem as scared as me.

"OK," I said quietly, and Jenny stepped forwards and squeezed me in a hug.

She and Dilip jumped out the room and I could hear Granny asking them, "What's all this plotting and planning?"

Quickly, I flipped through the pile of OS maps, glancing over the one on which Greystanes was marked. There was a fold-up map of the City of London, too. I shoved it in my pocket—just in case. On my way out the room, I placed the crisp packet carefully in the bin. And then I dashed to eat pancakes and listen to Granny telling a story that would take my mind off Dilip's claims, and off the night ahead.

8

THE WAY

We waited in bed until the house was quiet. Shortly before 11 o'clock, we tiptoed down the corridor to the boot room, slipping on trainers and pulling jogging pants and jackets over our chequered pyjamas. As we crossed the dome hallway to the Drawing Room, I got the same sailing feeling in my chest as I did before cricket trials.

The tiger rug lay still and lifeless. Dilip tiptoed over and hugged its raised head. Kneeling low, he began to whisper. The curtains flapped a little as if there was a breeze. I held my breath and watched as the tiger began to shimmer and move. I kept watching as its eyes and face and limbs began to glow and pulse with life, right there in front of us, stretching and yawning as usual. It licked around its shining teeth.

"It's time," said Dilip.

I was still not convinced that our plan, or lack of plan, would work. I fiddled with the folded map in my pocket.

"But what if…?" I had so many 'what ifs' I didn't know where to start. "Maybe we should talk about the journey? Maybe we should map the route first and plan our stops on the way… maybe?"

The tiger grunted. Tigers say 'Yes' or 'No', they never say 'Maybe'.

Dilip shrugged.

"It's time to go, Lal."

I gave up—I couldn't exactly argue with a tiger. The clock on the mantelpiece struck eleven. I checked this against my digital wristwatch, fingertips sweating as I fiddled to match up the times: 23:00hrs. Dilip hiccupped. He was gulping in air as if he was gulping back guava juice; he always did that when he was nervous. The hiccups broke the tension, at least. I opened the glass doors and let the tiger step out ahead of us into the cool, bright night. Jenny, waiting as planned, came rushing up, pockets bulging.

"Hi everyone. I brought some snacks."

"Good idea," I whispered. The tiger crouched. I helped the others on. Jenny sat up front with Dilip in the middle and I pulled myself up on to the tail end. Now that the tiger was in animal form again, its fur wasn't dull and worn. It was glossy and almost loose enough to grip to in patches.

"We're on," I said and patted the tiger. It rose to its feet, its back swaying from side to side. A metre isn't very high until you're on the back of a tiger. I felt on top of the world.

"It's like horse riding!" Jenny said. And it was—we'd been pony trekking in India on holiday once, and the tiger's gait wasn't so different. Its back, though, from its broad shoulder blades, was surprisingly narrow and bonier at the ridge than a pony's.

"I feel like Shakti," Dilip whispered.

"Shakti is a goddess of power in Hindu stories," I explained to Jenny. "She fights battles on the back of a tiger." You're not supposed to say you feel like a god, but I knew what Dilip meant—it was powerful and elegant.

Now in the garden, the tiger padded stealthily to the grass edge, barely leaving a pug mark on the soft ground. The tiger followed the curving hedge round to the Hidden Garden. It was late at night, but still light outside. In India it would have been pitch black at this hour, but here, in this queer country, the sun hadn't long set, the sky was still a watery blue. Clouds streaked across it like white arrows.

The Hidden Garden looked different in twilight. Pale shadows lurked, there were splashes in the pond and rustlings in the bushes—night creatures and frogs going about their ways. Jenny would be jumpy normally, and Dilip might have whimpered, but neither of them made a sound. The tiger stepped into the middle of the garden and onto the stone circle. I didn't want to offend, but didn't it know the way out? The gate was at Treehouse Corner end, not here in the tangled vegetable patch.

"Shall I guide you to the gate?" I asked. "It leads to the road."

The tiger's ears pricked back and it made a noise a bit like an engine revving, a noise that didn't sound friendly.

"We're not going by road," said Dilip.

58

"But there really isn't any other way out of town from here—there's nothing behind our house except woods and hills."

The tiger swung its head round and huffed gruffly.

"The road isn't the only way out of town," Dilip replied. I started to protest, not knowing yet how wise the tiger was, how wide its magic.

"But I looked at Mr. Stirling's maps," I insisted, "and the road is the only way."

The tiger gave a clipped purr, a big cat's way of telling you to keep your distance. I piped down, wobbling as the tiger edged its hind backwards and sank its head down into its shoulders. We tensed inwards with elbows and ankles. The big cat twitched in this position for a few long moments as though about to pounce on some imaginary prey. Its haunches trembled. And suddenly, swiftly, it sprang forwards, pushing with strong back legs, and we tucked in our knees and held our breath as up we went—and up, and up and up.

I gasped; my tummy somersaulted, and I curled inwards to Dilip, daring only to look with squinted eyes. Up above the houses, above streets, the school, the fields, we flew. We were so high that the farms below looked like Dilip's toy farm, then like Jenny's picture books, then like a dream. I pressed my lips closed against the cold air.

"Look! Look at the tiger!" Jenny screeched.

I didn't need to look—I could feel it, the tiger

transforming. This time, it was morphing from underneath us, levelling out to a rug again. It was hair-raisingly scary, but our palms stayed firm and flat against the thick, streaked skin. Jenny laughed out, "A magic carpet!" and she gathered us in close to the middle. I'd never thought of her as all that brave before—she was always squealing and gasping. Then an image of Jenny at the top of an evergreen flashed by, and I remembered she hadn't freaked out when seeing the tiger for the first time. And now, here she was, here we all were, flying. Flying into dimming light, far from ground, and not knowing where we were going. Our grins were pulled back as we rushed onwards, and my eyes started to sting with tears, even though I wasn't sad or sorry or sore.

"Close your eyes!" I called to the others, but my words were snatched and tossed by the wind. I bent in closer. "Close your eyes! The wind is so strong!" And we closed our eyes. And we flew, blind as bats, into the night.

9

WATERLOO

"Lal! Jenny! We've landed! Wake up, we've landed!"

Underneath us was hard, cold ground. The tiger skin rug stretched across our shoulders, its head in the shadows, eyes still. I looked up blearily to an empty railway platform and then up to the roof, a structure of white metal beams and glass panes streaked with pigeon droppings. At the far end of the platform was an unopened ticket office and an empty café, chairs stacked up and chained together to stop them being taken by thieves or the wind.

On a huge signpost, blue with round, white letters, it read:

Welcome to London Waterloo

I pushed against Dilip and pointed. "London! Waterloo Station! We made it! We're in London!" We shook Jenny awake.

She beamed sleepily, pulling her shoulders up and nodding, "Yes, it's London all right."

It was early, but the sun was up. The first train would arrive soon. Passengers would pour onto the platforms.

"We should get going," I said. "Shall we wake the tiger?" Dilip and Jenny shrugged. They always expected me to know what to do when they didn't, and then called me bossy when I told them—even though Jenny was the bossy one. I had no idea what to do with a live tiger in the middle of London. Maybe it was best to keep him as a rug for now. We sat there a bit longer.

Rustling in her pockets, Jenny brought out some squashed squares of tablet and three caramel wafer biscuits. They tasted supreme—buttery, chocolatey—but made me feel very far from the pantry at Greystanes filled with Naniji's Indian sweets and spices.

"What about the tiger?" Jenny asked. "I'll save my last bite for him."

"The tiger is magic, silly. He doesn't need to eat. And anyway, tigers don't like chocolate biscuits, they like frizzy-haired girls!" The platform echoed with Dilip's twittering laughter, and then with another sound. Footsteps.

The footsteps were steady and coming closer. A large man in uniform stepped into sight.

"Well, hello, what have we here, eh?" he said in an impatient tone, and then answered his own question with, "Three delinquent children, that's what. Just what I need first thing in the morning."

Jenny shuffled to the side, cleverly hiding the tiger's drooping head.

"Lal, who is he?" Dilip asked a bit too loudly. "What did he call us?"

"For your information, kiddo," the man said gruffly, "I am the Station Customer Services Manager. The question here is, who are you?"

Dilip's hiccups came back. Jenny let out this weird, gaspy giggle. Her face went blotchy pink. The man grew more gnarly.

"Oh, I see, so you're the cheeky sort, are you? And here's me thinking you needed help."

I stood up to be polite to the Customer-Manager-Whatsit, who didn't seem very customer friendly. I pulled on Jenny to stand up, too, and she yanked Dilip to his feet.

"Sorry, sir," I said. (In India, we called grown-up men 'sir', even and sometimes especially the mean ones). "My brother was just wondering what you meant by 'delinquent', sir. I think it—"

"It means 'criminal'," he cut me off, "and what *I'd* like to know is what *crime* you three are running away from."

I tried to speak, but it was like a bullfrog was stuck in my throat. Dilip hiccupped and Jenny giggle-gasped again. The man broadened his shoulders and fixed his shirt cuffs self-importantly.

"Right-oh. You're all coming with me to the police station."

"But we haven't done anything wrong!" Jenny was outraged.

The man ignored her, and pointed to the tiger skin, not looking close enough to see its striped print or its head in the shadows.

"Bring your belongings with you. Come on." We looked at each other and at the rug. We couldn't leave the tiger in the middle of the station. "What are you waiting for?" barked the man, pacing ahead.

"Let's try carrying it," whispered Jenny, picking up one corner. Dilip crouched to take up another corner. How could we carry it and hide what it was? I lifted up its head by the chin. It wasn't heavy, just super awkward. I tried covering it with my jacket. Dilip's corner sagged and it was tricky to walk in sync. Jenny tripped and dropped her end and Dilip let go.

The Customer Services Manager turned and stamped back towards us.

"Come on, hurry up. What's that you've got, eh? What's in that bundle? Things you've nicked, is it? And now you've been caught you think you can stash it all on my platform, eh?"

My fist clenched around the tiger, but it was Jenny who launched in.

"No, that's mean! We weren't leaving it and we haven't stolen anything!" she cried. "You've got it all wrong!"

The manager whipped around at her; Jenny cowered into me and squealed as if the man was going to strike her or something awful. But before he could do anything, the tiger, quicker than a blink, roared up from the cold floor into its full, frightening form and growled at the hulking man. The man yelled out and ran, like a cartoon villain, all the way to the ticket office, where we heard him bolting himself inside.

Jenny steadied herself and then she grabbed me in one of her suffocating squeezes. She hugged Dilip, too, and started kissing the tiger's whiskery face. "Oh, thank you!" she kept saying. "I got such a fright. Thank you!"

The tiger bowed its head, but its tail was flicking at the end. I scanned the station to check there was nobody else around. The Customer Services Manager was probably calling the cops… there wasn't time to stand around hugging. The tiger prowled forwards, sniffing the air. Daylight. City noises. It padded to the edge of the platform. Follow me, it seemed to be commanding. I couldn't agree more—it was time to get back on track.

10

IN A TANGLE

We kept close to the tiger. At the platform edge it jumped, strong-limbed, to the railway line. We lowered ourselves down and trotted after it along the thick tracks to two parked trains, following in single file between their carriages.

We reached the far end of the trains where the track opened out to a sunny day. At first the city was still and sleepy, but now there was clattering, chattering and revving, sounds of people and buses, cars and bicycles. London was waking up.

The track was set high on a walled bridge above street level. Tall buildings with big windows looked over it, so there was nowhere to hide. The Customer Services Manager would definitely have called the police by now, I thought. Or the zoo, or maybe the newspapers?

Suddenly, one of the train engines heaved and spluttered. The tiger tensed its neck upwards and sniffed the air. It flashed forwards, bounded once over a metal fire escape bolted on to the wall, and disappeared over the other side.

"Quickly," I hissed, and we scrambled across and down the escape ladder. The ladder didn't reach the ground, so we had to jump, avoiding landing in oily puddles. Dilip tapped me on the shoulder. He looked like he was about to cry. I looked to Jenny. "Where are we?"

"Nowhere I know," she shrugged. The tiger sniffed the air again and then delved to the shadows of an archway under the bridge. We followed it, but from the dark, the tiger urged us with its nose back out. We stood in the square of concreted ground, fenced in with barbed wire. I looked to the tiger for more instructions, but it had slunk back into the dark.

Beyond the fence and across the road was a grubby café offering hot food. My tummy grumbled. Of course—it was breakfast time.

"Guys, I think the tiger's telling us it's time to eat," I said, pushing on a rickety gate that opened onto the street. We scurried across the road like mice to a block of cheese.

Inside, the café smelled of bacon. A skinny lady appeared behind a display of greasy pies and stodgy cakes, wiping her hands on her apron.

"Something to eat?"

Jenny pointed at items listed on a well-used laminate

menu and we nodded in agreement.

"Three fried egg rolls, three strawberry tarts and three cans of cola," she said.

"Got the cash to pay for this, do you?" replied the lady, looking us up and down.

Jenny nodded, raking together enough pocket money to cover the order. We sat on tall stools and leaned against the table bar that ran the length of the window. When breakfast arrived, I wolfed mine down so fast my belly ached. It was just what we'd needed. Stretching, I looked at the time on my wristwatch: 08:00hrs.

It was early, but there was no time to relax. Across the road and under the archway, the tiger was in hiding. Now that it was out of Greystanes, it seemed wilder, somehow, and although it was looking after us, it was sort of up to us to look after it, too.

I looked down the street, along its strip of shops. There was a laundry service, a betting store with closed shutters, a beauty parlour with a sign flashing 'NAILZ' in neon, and a boarded-up business. Slowly, it dawned on me why the tiger had brought us here, to this street. It wasn't for breakfast. The tiger had been here before. Above the shut-up shop were the faded words,

'JOSEPH ECKS AUCTIONEERS'.

I pointed out the sign to the others and Jenny read the

name to Dilip, who nearly fell of his stool.

"Woah! Is it really J. Ecks, Lal?"

"Yup—let's check this out," I said, scraping my stool back to stand up. Jenny dusted crumbs off Dilip and ordered him to go and wash his sticky face. She had strawberry sauce on her face, too, and her hair looked like a bird's nest. We were filthy. It was no wonder the lady at the counter had raised her eyebrows at us—or that the Customer Services man had thought we were nothing but trouble. We left the café.

Although I recognised it from the pictures, the shop wasn't as colourful as it had looked online. Or as open. It was early, but Ecks didn't look like it had been open in a long time or like was opening again any time soon. Circles of white paint smeared the windows, and through the gaps in the markings we could see a ladder inside, bare walls, and some cardboard boxes on the floor. Behind the counter was a wooden cabinet with a few odd things inside—silverware, a porcelain clown, and a clock. The clock was like the one in the Drawing Room at Greystanes. Time was ticking on and all we had found was a derelict shop.

Jenny whistled through her teeth. "What do we do?"

"Ask someone?" I replied. "The neighbours might know where Joseph Ecks is now."

The launderette and the betting shop weren't open yet, but NAILZ had a dim light on inside. The sign read

'Closed' but there was a shadow of someone moving about in there. I knocked on the glass. No answer. Jenny was bolder; she stepped up and turned the door handle. As she pushed the door open, a bell tinkled and clinked somewhere above.

An exposed bulb dangled from the ceiling. Two tables were set up for manicures, and a whole corner of the parlour was dedicated to wigs and hair extensions. A poster advertised prices for 'Afro Stylz'. Bunting, printed in Caribbean flags mixed with the Union Jack, decked one wall. From behind a beaded curtain at the back of the shop, a large woman wearing an orange dress appeared, bottom first, walking backwards. She was carrying a tray and when she turned around and saw us, she nearly dropped it.

"Oh!" she shrieked. "I didn't know you were here! I didn't hear the door!" Her accent matched the bunting, like it came from a mixture of places. "Sorry, sorry, I was gettin' me a cup of tea," and she put the tray down precariously on a pile of beauty magazines. "Now, what are you doin' here?" she asked, fixing her twisted headscarf. "We're not open yet, you know. How can I be helpin' you?"

"Um, we were wondering about the old auction place," Jenny managed. "If you knew where the man is now."

"Joseph Ecks," I added. "We need to find him."

The woman trapped me in a hard stare as she backed her rear side onto a salon chair. She was older than she first looked. Her skin gathered into wrinkles around her eyes and the hair peeking out from her headscarf was white.

"Well, well," she said softly. "Old Joe, as I called him. An old friend of mine." I squeezed my fists in anticipation. She looked up and said, "I'm afraid he can't help you. He died some years back."

The words were like nettle stings, sharp at first, then burning. Joseph Ecks was dead. How were we ever going to help the tiger now? I looked round at the others. The woman had stood up and bustled over to Jenny and was gently touching her hair.

"This hair is so nice, my child. Strands of gold, so beautiful. I'll brush it for you. Here, sit," and she manoeuvred Jenny, who had also been stung to silence, into the salon corner, sitting her down on a swivel chair in front of a mirror. She started picking with her thick fingers through Jenny's hair—which was more like straw than gold in my opinion. "So, what did you want with Old Joe?"

"He had something we need," I said carefully. The woman looked at me in the mirror as she spoke.

"Somet'ing you need, hey? And why d'you need that somet'ing?" her eyes sparkled. She produced a comb and worked it through Jenny's haystack.

"To help someone," Dilip said.

I pushed gently against Dilip's shoulders, not wanting him to give too much away. "And to help us get back home," he added. The hairdresser stopped combing Jenny's hair and looked up at Dilip and then to me like she knew us.

"Get back home? Are you lost?"

"No, just homesick."

"Well, then. Somet'ing that will get you closer to home is a good somet'ing." She sighed. "I'm homesick, too. I haven't made it to my home yet."

"What do you mean?" asked Dilip. "Do you live in your shop?"

The woman cackled and her eyes danced. "No, child! I live in a regular house. But I haven't made it yet to *Africa*," and when she said the word her eyes expanded, bulging white, and the word sounded mystical. "*Africa* is my homeland." Her voice turned all preachy. "I was born in London. Born and bred. My parents moved here from Jamaica—which is where their great grandparents were sent to as slaves, from Africa, long ago. I'm a caterpillar in a chrysalis. One day I will get to visit my homeland, be a butterfly like I'm meant to be.

"Joe used to say I was already a butterfly, and all I needed was to spread my wings," and she chuckled to herself and tugged again at Jenny's hair. Jenny yelped. "Sorry, child. These hairs o' yours are a terrible tangle."

Everything was a terrible tangle. The truth was, we *were* lost. Impossibly lost. The hairdresser, who was tying Jenny's hair in a ponytail, seemed nothing like a butterfly to me.

"Well, you may still find what you need," she sighed. "Ecks shut up shop here years ago, months before he died, but his family opened a nice little gallery on Rye Road, in Peckham Rye. It's still there. His daughter owns it now." She shook her head and cackled again, saying, "Old Joe". She was a bit crazy, I thought, like a smiling crocodile. She waddled to the door and glanced at her mug on the tray. "My tea's gone cold." The bell clinked again as she held the door open.

The other two went ahead of me and just as I was stepping out, the hairdresser grabbed me by the upper arm. "Joe liked puzzles, you know, but he took the answers with him to the grave. You're not the only ones looking for answers." I must have looked frightened, because she let go and smiled. "Don't be disappointed, is all I'm sayin' to you."

I smiled briefly back and hurried away from her shop.

"Are you OK, Lal? What was that all about?" Jenny asked as we picked our way back to the tiger through litter and dandelions. "What did she mean, we're not the only ones looking for answers?"

I didn't reply, I was turning things over in my head. It was a relief to be out of NAILZ, but I had a lingering feeling that we weren't quite finished with that strange woman. Under the bridge, and from behind a pile of breeze-blocks, the tiger looked up eagerly. But when Dilip shook his head, its chin fell back to its paws.

11

ECKS MARKS THE SPOT

"We can't just give up," Jenny said, stroking the tiger. "I mean, what if Joe's daughter *knows* something?"

I'd been running my fingers along the papery spine of Mr. Stirling's map in my pocket.

"If the tiger stays here," I suggested, "we can go on our own to Peckham Rye and look for Ecks's gallery." I tugged out the map. "I brought this."

The tiger perked up immediately. It stretched and came right up to me and rubbed its head against my shoulder. I leaned into the feeling, which was the nicest I'd had since Mum had hugged me goodnight the evening before.

"It would be quickest to fly with the tiger," Jenny pointed out.

"We'd be caught," I said, pinning down the corners of the map with chunks of rubble.

"Can you imagine what people would say if they saw

a flying tiger?" Dilip beamed.

"Exactly," I replied sternly and looked on the map for Peckham Rye. It was on the same side of the river as we were and I guessed it was about an hour's walk at Dilip's pace.

"Well, can't we carry it?" Jenny asked.

"No, we tried that at the station. It's safer if it hides here."

"But what if we need its help?"

I looked at the tiger. It blinked and its ears folded backwards. Dilip whispered something to it and the tiger bowed its head.

"He will help us," Dilip said. "If we're stuck, I'll whisper for him and he will help us."

I didn't bother questioning him this time. I don't think Jenny trusted my map-reading, but she did trust the tiger. She scratched behind its ears and it meowed in a friendly, low tone almost like a cow mooing. We all smiled. I re-folded the map and nodded at the tiger.

"OK, let's go," I said, taking the lead. When we reached the fence, I turned to wave to the tiger from the edge of the shadow, but it was impossible to see it in the darkness.

Mr. Stirling's map was brilliant. Jenny and Dilip didn't have a clue how to read maps, but I loved that sort of thing. Ajay had given me a compass for my last birthday, and I wished I had it with me. Luckily, London streets are nicely signposted. And besides, it turned out there was another kind of map: the grid of the London Underground.

At the other side of Waterloo Station was a 'Tube' stop, the entrance to an underground world, a network of train lines below the city. I grabbed a free map from a pile at the counter when Jenny was buying tickets. People were rushing up and down the tiled corridors like a time-lapse movie. Corridors joined other corridors, met up with escalators and opened out into rail tunnels.

As we got onto a train on the Bakerloo Line, a tinny voice told us to "Mind the Gap", a dark drop between the platform and the track. The carriage had yellow plastic seats and swayed from side to side. Jenny found a seat and heaved Dilip onto her lap. I stood against a pole, and as we moved off I got the uneasy feeling we were heading in the wrong direction—north instead of south.

The train was busy with Saturday shoppers, tourists and business people. A man sat down a little further along and held up a double-spread of newspaper. Again, I imagined us making headlines ('Children Kidnapped by Tiger!'). But the cover story was about a refugee crisis, people fleeing to Europe to escape war and difficult lives. Mum and Baba had chosen to leave India; even though I hadn't wanted to go, I hadn't exactly been *forced* to leave.

I was staring blankly but blinked when the man turned the page and I caught a glimpse of the jacket on his lap. My heart lurched. The man was wearing black from head to toe, and from underneath the paper, which was hiding his face, I could see silver sequins in the shape of a snake's tail. It was him. *The man with the snake jacket was on the train.* He must be following us. Maybe he'd overheard our plans when we were in the treehouse. The train closed in on me. I pinched Jenny's arm and hissed at her.

"Go, go, get off at the next station." She stood up, alarmed, Dilip wobbling off her knee. I led them, ducking under people's arms and stepping over briefcases and bags, to the door. The man was also getting up. His face was hidden by other passengers, but I could see the silver of the snake moving towards us.

"What is it, Lal?"

"We're being followed," I said, and quickly explained.

The train stopped and the doors took ages to open. We jumped into the jostling crowd and squeezed, hand-in-hand, through mobs of people. I checked back again and saw we were gaining distance from the snake man, who had rolled up his newspaper like a mast as he tried to make his way through the sea of people. We bent double and hurried to the nearest escalator. I saw him get caught in the crowd, and as the escalator went up, he shrank out of sight.

Emerging from below the city, we exited through the station turnstiles, passing a coffee kiosk and a flower stall, great big bunches in full bloom. "Great big prices," Baba would have said, but I forced the thought of Baba away.

Behind the stall were some trees. They made a perfect hiding place—we dived towards them and sat on the damp grass to catch our breath.

"That was definitely him, Lal," Dilip's voice was too loud. "Do you think he wants to get the rug from us?"

"Shhh," I said, checking the station.

"There he is! Isn't that him?" Dilip cried out. The man, who was holding up his newspaper to shield the morning glare, had appeared from behind barrels of roses. I elbowed Dilip and he yelped, "Ow!"

"Shhh!"

The man looked over, but we were well hidden and kept still. My breathing was heavy and sweat tickled and itched my neck. The man was looking around. I bit my lips and got the metallic taste of blood. The man turned away, jogged up the steps and was gone.

The name of the station was 'Embankment'. I unfolded the map and found it, north across the river along the brown Bakerloo Line. "Argh! I knew it—we've gone the wrong way."

"At least we led the man in the snake jacket in the

wrong direction, too," Jenny said, and it was true. I studied the maps a bit more, figuring out where to go. We had to get back on the Bakerloo Line and get off at a station weirdly called 'Elephant and Castle'—from there, we'd catch an overland train. The expedition was turning out to take much longer than I'd estimated.

"OK, I have a plan. Stick with me. Let's go."

We slipped from behind the flower cart back into the station and caught the next train. "This is it!" I said as we reached our stop, cajoling the others out and checking we weren't being followed.

This time we exited onto the edge of a screeching intersection where there was a big statue with peeling paint—an elephant with a castle on its back. It reminded me of Indian stories when elephants carried princes on howdahs, those big seats with sun-shading canopies. Princes or rich people, bobbing about to show off or setting out to hunt tigers. At the thought of tiger hunting, the fire in me flared up again. So did indigestion from our greasy breakfast.

We made our way to the station along a line of trees that Jenny called 'London planes'. After we'd got tickets from a machine, we boarded an overland train for Peckham Rye.

"So, what do we do when we get there?" Jenny looked at me. "And where exactly is the gallery?"

"She said it was on Rye Road..." I unfolded the map

and found it. It was a long road.

"We don't even know the gallery name," Jenny said unhelpfully.

"We can ask someone," Dilip suggested.

As it happened, we didn't have to. I led us out the station to the corner of Rye Road and would have spotted it first if I hadn't had my nose in the map. Jenny did one of her squeals.

"There! Look over there!" One block down, in a row of low, redbrick buildings sat a little shop freshly painted in white and lime with *Gallery Ecks* printed in fine, black writing. "Ecks marks the spot!" Jenny laughed, jumping up and down.

Inside, the gallery was spacious. Giant scribbles in frames were fixed to its white walls. Sculptures shaped like rude body bits balanced on pedestals. In a corner, a petite woman with mousy brown hair and big tortoiseshell glasses looked up from her chair.

"Hello, can I help you?"

"Eh... Yes, we're, eh, looking, um, for, well, we're not sure. We need to, um, find out something," I stammered and Jenny coughed to hide a snigger.

"Something?" smiled the woman. "What sort of something?" My neck pulsed—what sort of something?

"Well," I managed to say, "it's something that Joseph Ecks might have been able to help with." I didn't know what else to say. The woman leaned forwards on her toes.

"Joseph Ecks? He was my grandfather." She smiled. "I'm Jo, too—but it's short for Joanna."

I grinned. Her grandfather was J. Ecks, Auctioneer.

"Well, we were there, at his old place," I stammered. "But it's all shut up and we need something, you see. To know something. About a tiger. That is, about a tiger skin rug."

When Joanna stood up, she wasn't much taller than me. She swept around me with silk-sleeved arms like bird wings and steered me on to her chair. She poured a small tumbler of water and said, "Take a sip and a deep breath. Tell me exactly what it is you want to know about a tiger skin rug," and she pushed her glasses up her nose. When my voice came back, Joanna listened intently, rotating her head like an owl as I talked. I told her that her grandfather had sold a tiger skin rug, that we needed to know where it came from, and that it was urgent.

When I stopped talking, Joanna paced with light, excited steps.

"Well," she pushed up her glasses again. "I do know about a tiger skin rug. My grandfather only ever sold one, so it must be the one you want to know about." Jenny and I exchanged hopeful looks. "It was one of my favourite stories when I was a girl. You see, when it arrived in his shop from India—it came from India, but I'm not sure where—it had a little pouch around its neck. And there was a box inside the pouch." I took another sip of water, swallowing loudly. "The odd thing was," she continued, "nobody could open the box. It was tight shut. Grandad Joe tried for years. The box wouldn't open. We never found out what was inside it."

"What did he do with it, your grandad?" Jenny asked. We'd all leaned forwards.

"Well, he sold the rug—it went up to Scotland, I think. But he kept the box for himself. He thought maybe there was something valuable inside it. It was rather beautiful. It had a butterfly painted on it."

"Where is it now? Do you have it?" Jenny asked, but Joanna shook her head.

"No." Her mouth twisted to the side. "I always wished we'd kept it, but he gave it away, in return for a riddle. It was so like Grandad Joe to do that sort of thing. He lost money that way when he got older—he would auction things off for the best riddle or sell them for a song. That's why my mother opened this gallery—the family business would have been ruined otherwise. But yes, I do remember, he gave that box away."

"Who did he give it to, Miss?" my voice crackled. "Do you know who he gave it to?"

"Yes, yes I do. It was to a friend of his called Angela. She ran a beauty parlour next door to his auction house. But I doubt she's still there—it was always her dream to move to Africa."

There was a pause and then Jenny screeched. "The hairdresser lady? From NAILZ? But she is still there!" and she started jabbering that we'd met her that same morning. I got up from the chair. Dilip was leaping about so much that Joanna put on a voice like a cross cricket coach to say Please Don't Knock into the Artwork.

"What do you know about that tiger skin rug, anyway?" she asked, looking at me with piercing eyes. "Why are you looking for my grandfather's little box?"

Her grandfather's box? It wasn't his, it was the tiger's. Her family had sort of stolen it. We shouldn't tell her anything. Plus, she was probably no different to any other grown-ups, living in a world where the tiger could never be real. "What do you need to know this for?" she asked again. Dilip opened his mouth to speak, but I pulled on his sleeve.

"It's a school project," Jenny lied, going blotchy. Joanna looked doubtful and I wished Jenny wasn't such a rubbish fibber.

"In the summer holidays?" Joanna raised an eyebrow. "Come on, tell me, I'm curious—what do you know about the rug? How do you know about it?"

"Thanks for your help," I replied, "but we really have to go now." We hurried to the door, Dilip accidentally catching his foot on a display stand. Joanna dashed to stop the sculpture on top from wobbling off.

"Wait!" she called after us, unable to move as she

84

propped up the ceramic. As soon as we were out on the street again, I told the others to keep walking. At the corner, Dilip turned to look back.

"She's there, Lal," he said, giving a meek little wave. I saw Joanna perched at the lime green door and, guiltily, I turned away.

12

THE BUTTERFLY BOX

The next train was in ten minutes, leaving enough time to buy a bag of sweets at the train station shop. Nobody said much on the ride, not even Jenny, as we sat scoffing strawberry bonbons. What if Angela no longer had the box? What if someone had discovered the tiger? I tried to push the big questions away, to concentrate instead on the immediate journey, the task at hand, the bits of pink candy stuck in my teeth. Dilip was kicking his legs against the chair.

"Didn't the hairdresser say something about Ecks liking puzzles or something?" he sucked back sugar. "That he took the answers with him?"

"Yeah," Jenny sat up. "She must have meant the box. Imagine all this time she hasn't been able to open it. That would drive anyone loopers. There must be something very special inside it."

Yes, there was something special inside it. I was 99%

sure it was the message. And if we got it, we could help the tiger deliver it and keep its promise. Then it would help get us back to India and everything would be back to normal.

Like most journeys, this one felt shorter on the way back.

This time, the salon wasn't empty. Two women sat at the manicure table, one sticking fake jewels on to the other's electric-blue fingernails. Someone was sitting in the hairdressing chair with a cloak on and clips in her hair. They all swung their heads around when we went in. Angela burst out from behind the beaded curtain.

"Well, well, well," she cackled. "I see y'are back again to see me. Did you find what you were lookin' for?" She unclasped butterfly clips from her customer's hair.

"Not quite," I replied. "We found the gallery, but Joanna Ecks told us that you, Angela, might have what we need." Angela didn't flinch at my use of her name. She fluffed up the hair she'd worked on and began spraying it from an aerosol that smelled like perfume mixed with mosquito repellent.

"Mm hmm," she wiggled her hips and took out a mirror, angling it up to show the client her new style. The heads at the manicure table had turned back to nail varnish and gossip. We waited while Angela uncloaked her customer, settled her bill, and swept the floor. She seemed purposefully unhurried. At last, she adjusted her headdress, looked herself up and down in the mirror approvingly, and turned, one fist on her hip.

"Look 'ere. The only t'ing Old Joe ever gave me, of all the precious t'ings in dat shop, was a box that can't be opened. All those priceless t'ings, and I got me a shut box. Now don't go telling me that it's that old box y'are after?" She looked directly at me, eyes glinting.

"Yes, ma'am," I confirmed, "we're looking for that box."

Angela's eyes bulged. She threw her head back in a crazed laugh. The faces from the manicure table turned briefly. "Joe always said someone would come back lookin' for it. And here y'are! But why should I give it to three little kids?" Her voice lowered to a rusty whisper and she leaned in, hands on her hips. "Someone else came for it, you know."

Someone else?

"When?" I asked.

"Ah, years ago. When Joe had it. Wanted that, and to know the whereabouts of the tiger skin rug it came with." The smile had gone from Angela's face.

"What? Who? Who came for it?"

"I don't know who. Someone from India. A man," she said in a low voice. "But don't you worry, Joe sent him packin'." I swallowed hard. "Anyway," Angela continued, "there ain't no openin' that box. It's locked tight shut. Not even a drill would chip it." She paused, then asked,

"What would you give to see it?"

I stifled a gulp. She had on the sly crocodile smile again. We needed the box. What would she take for it? What, after all, was it worth? What was it worth to Angela? And then I remembered what Joanna had said about her grandfather giving it away for a riddle. Would Angela give it to us if she got back what she'd paid for it?

She was breathing heavily. I scanned the room for an idea, an answer. I saw the clips she'd taken out of her client's hair and remembered what Joanna had said about the box—and what Old Joe had said about Angela. Suddenly, I was blurting out a rhyme, making it up as I went. "*I have lots of legs and then I die... I have six legs, and then I fly...*" Jenny and Dilip were looking at me in confusion, but Angela had cocked her head and we locked eyes as I finished the riddle... "*What am I?*"

Angela cackled again and, flashing her sparkling teeth, repeated, "I have lots of legs and then I die, I have six legs and then I fly."

I'd made it up on the spot, but it was working like a charm. Angela pursed her deep, red lips together.

"Come with me," she nodded and walked out the salon through the beaded curtain. We stood where we were. The manicurist looked up from her diamanté work.

"On you go," she said, and I led the way.

13

THE MESSAGE

The back room turned out to be a small hallway. There was a cluttered kitchenette and some steep spiral steps. Angela had reached the top.

"Up here!" she called. The steps were wooden and speckled with old paint. The room at the top was full to the brim with mannequins, wigs and hairpieces, boxes of dyes and beads. It smelled of packaging and shampoo. Dilip came up last, pushing us forwards and into Angela, who was bent, backside up, into a trunk. "All right, all right!" she crowed, heaving herself up. "Here it is."

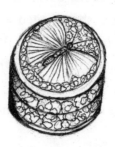

She turned around dangling a pull-string bag. She emptied its contents into my palm. A small box. I'd never seen anything like it. Small and round, with a flat base and curved top, it was made of wood and paper mâché and hand-painted in turquoise and indigo. The pattern was of a butterfly.

"That's the answer to your riddle, isn't it?" she asked. "A butterfly?" and there was a flutter up my spine. The painted butterfly glinted as I turned it in my hand. Its wings touched the edges of the lid, which was fastened together with a simple triangular groove. How difficult could it be to open that?

"I tell you what," bargained Angela. "You're not getting my beautiful butterfly box. It was the one t'ing my old friend ever gave me. But if you can open it, you can keep whatever it is inside," and her eyes flashed across us. Jenny was on tiptoes with excitement.

I sat the box squarely in my palm, cupped my hands around it tightly, and pulled. I tried again, pulling harder. I was trying to lift the lid off, but it was strongly and strangely magnetised to the base. It didn't budge. Jenny waved her fingers for a go. I tried a third time, pulling till my knuckles went white. Jenny took the box. Holding it sideways, she tried to twist the pieces apart. Her cheeks reddened, and she puffed out, giving up. It was too tight.

Angela shrugged. "I told you children not to get your hopes up."

"Want a shot?" Jenny held the mysterious box out to Dilip. "Give it a try."

Dilip took it carefully between his small fingers. He turned it round and round. All eyes were on him, but he wasn't rushing. Angela cleared her throat, but still he took his time. Then he lowered his chin, drew the box up to his lips, closed his eyes and began to whisper. He whispered for the tiger. Of course—it had told us that if we got stuck, Dilip should whisper for its help. And we were definitely stuck—as stuck as the lid of that box.

Cold, dim air gusted around the room, bringing with it a gentle sound like glockenspiels playing far, far away. Dilip stopped whispering. He handed me the box back and the light in the room lifted.

This time, when I tried to part the small circular lid from the base, it came away easily with a soft 'pop'. I handed the lid to Angela, who took it with a look of total disbelief. Inside, couched on a small rag of cloth, was a gold ring. I pinched around it and folded it quickly into my fist, offering the base to Angela. She bowed her head as she took it.

"Thank you," I said.

"Well, well, well," she muttered, looking at the two parts. "I'm sorry Old Joe wasn't here to witness that." She frowned towards Dilip. "Strength isn't always what we think it is, now is it?" and, with a low cackle, she turned her back on us and delved back into her trunk.

We retreated carefully but quickly down the steps, away from Angela, in case she changed her mind and wanted to keep the ring, too. She kept on muttering, "Well, well, well, if Old Joe had seen that…"

As we crossed the parlour on the way out, the women at the manicure table didn't even look up.

The tiger's dark figure in the shadows came closer and its whiskers caught the daylight. When I held out the ring, it narrowed its eyes. A tiger's mouth, when resting, dips down and up like it's smiling. But this time, the tiger really smiled. It opened its mouth and its tongue hung out and its whisker-pads inched upwards.

Under the archway, we cuddled into the warm cat and took turns at examining the ring. Although the outer ring was plain, the inside was engraved with a delicate chain of flowers, fastened together with fancy script.

"Look, there's some cryptic writing," Jenny said, squinting in the dim light. "It must be code."

I took the ring from her and held it to the light.

"That's not code," I smiled at Dilip. "It's Hindi."

"What? What does it say?" yelped Dilip.

"It says, *Menon Chatterjee, from Mother*," I translated.

"That's the message?" asked Jenny.

"I guess we have to give it to a man called Menon Chatterjee, from his mum?" I said, not wanting to admit it seemed vaguely disappointing. The tiger was pushing me with its forehead. "Yes?" I asked. "Is that what we have to do?"

"Yes," Dilip responded excitedly. "The tiger says yes."

We had it, the message. A real name and a real offering. I passed the ring around once more. It fitted on Jenny's finger, and we agreed it was a pretty safe place for it, even though I hesitated when handing it over.

"We need to find out who he is. Where's the nearest Internet spot?" Jenny wondered, glancing up towards the station. "We're *no way* going back to Waterloo," she shuddered. "We'll stay here with the tiger, Lal. You'll be faster finding somewhere on your own." She emptied into my palm the last of her pocket money.

I set off down the road. A short walk from the tunnel, I came across 'Everything Express', offering cheap dry cleaning, key cutting, shoe polishing, passport photographs and Internet. I ordered twenty minutes of browsing time and got to work.

Pulling up a swivel stool in front of a computer, I typed, 'Menon Chatterjee.' First on the search-engine list was a website called 'nameyourbabybunting.com'. I clicked on a few more sites—an actor, a poet, lots of links to social media. Anything else? The connection in Everything Express was slower than a three-toed sloth; nearly five minutes had gone.

I spent five more tapping into the keyboard and

scrolling down search returns. Nothing sprung out at me. After everything—following clues, getting the ring, discovering a name—surely we couldn't fail at finding out who the name belonged to? I wriggled my fingers above the keys. Who *was* Menon Chatterjee? The same person Ecks had 'sent packing'? Or someone else? I needed a better list…

And then I remembered it. Baba's database. I typed it in: *The Hindus' Who's Who of Who's Here.* Up popped his website. It was a clunky name, but the thing was a masterpiece. Totally mind boggling. Baba had crafted a detailed table of Indian names. I typed in 'Chatterjee' and, after a small amount of churning, a list appeared. There were several Menon Chatterjees. I read each entry carefully. There was a retired doctor, a magazine editor, and an obituary for someone who'd been a 'pillar of the community'. One Menon Chatterjee was a professor at Coventry University. His entry had a link to the professor's university homepage. I clicked on it and a new tab came up.

At the top of the page was a banner of rotating pictures—students smiling at books on desks, students smiling at each other on benches, students smiling into microscopes. I skimmed down and stared at the image of a bearded and bespectacled Indian man. The man in the profile picture stared straight back at me. The blurb at the side had me on the edge of the swivel stool.

**Menon Chatterjee, Professor of Conservation
and Biodiversity. Main research interests include
molecular ecology and conservation of endangered
mammals, with a specific focus on Indian and East
Asian mammals. Outreach includes projects in
India and with breeding programmes across Europe
relating to all subspecies of tiger.**

Of tiger. *Tiger*. My fingers froze above the board. Was
I reading this right? It couldn't be coincidence. Had I
seriously just found who we were looking for? And on
Baba's unpronounceable website?

I re-read the paragraph, slowly this time, and clicked
on 'List of Publications'. A long list of titles appeared of
articles the professor had written on the conservation
of Indian and East Asian wildcats. It must be the same
person, surely it must?

A message popped up: ONE MINUTE REMAINING.
Flustered, I was trying to get to the 'Contact Details'
section, but before I could, the screen turned blue and
a ribbon of white letters read, TIME OUT! TIME OUT!
TIME OUT!

As I made my way back to the others, I couldn't
shake the smiling man with his big beard from my head.
Conservation and Biodiversity. Coventry University. I
kicked a concrete breeze-block. I should have got more
information.

When I arrived back, the tiger was pacing again. Jenny shot up when she saw me.

"The man was here, Lal," she said. "The one with the snake jacket. I saw someone and thought it was you coming back."

"But you walked past, so I went running out," said Dilip, "but all I saw was the man's back—it was the silver snake, Lal. He was going towards NAILZ."

Blood pounded in my temples. The tiger was getting agitated too, its tail twitching at the end. "Well, he won't find anything there," I said. I wondered if he was looking for the message, or just for us?

"What did you find, Lal? About Chatterjee?" Jenny asked, and when I told them about the professor, Jenny jumped up and down. "We have to go Coventry!"

I looked at the tiger. Flying in daylight seemed a crazy idea. The tiger stopped pacing and made a long, low groaning sound.

"It can take us there, we're not going to get lost," said Dilip.

"I know," I snapped. It wasn't getting lost that worried me. It was being spotted in broad daylight. And that we'd already been away for so long, not to mention that we were being followed.

"And flying with the tiger will shake off the snake man," said Jenny.

Trains rumbled overhead. People were walking by,

probably wondering what three kids were doing kicking about behind a railway fence. There were empty cans on the ground and someone's old pizza box. It was simple luck we hadn't been discovered under this arch yet, and the tiger was clearly not happy.

We climbed on to its back. The ride was less swift than the night before. The tiger moved jaggedly along the rail bridge and behind a tall office block facing the sun—all the window blinds were drawn. On take-off, the tiger sprung almost vertically without much warning, so we slipped back and I had to grab on extra tight. I thought we'd got away unseen when I spotted the gaping face of a crane driver, sitting in his little box. He rubbed his eyes as if he didn't believe what he was seeing, and then we were gone. When we'd surged high above the city, the tiger flattened into a rug again.

As it flattened, I noticed its stripes weren't only on its fur—the pigment seeped deep into its skin. I wished again that I could talk to it like Dilip did.

Flying was even more exciting by day. Below us, a long river, like a python, ran across grids of concrete and stone. Somewhere down there was the mysterious man. And Gallery Ecks. I imagined Joanna looking up and waving to us as we flew over. I spotted the Houses of Parliament—their spiky parapets—the London Eye, and Big Ben, the famous clock. I closed my eyes, trying not to think about time and how it was supposed to be taking care of itself. Nearly a whole day had gone and who knew what havoc we'd raised at Greystanes. At least we were one step closer to helping the tiger, I told myself. At least we were one step closer to home.

14

THE PROFESSOR'S NOTE

It was early afternoon when we reached Coventry. Stuffy road fumes wrapped around us, but wild air from the flight still buzzed in our ears. Avoiding the busy centre and main roads, the tiger flew low to the ground behind supermarkets and metal warehouses. None of us uttered a word. As if we were on a haunted ride at a funfair, I half-expected a skeleton to spring out from behind a wheelie bin.

At the gates to a large post office depot we narrowly missed a horde of workers scattering out from their shifts. The tiger swerved and delved into a narrow street to avoid them. But halfway down the street, a postman was kneeling, rummaging in his parcel bag. Sharply, the tiger skidded into a tight alleyway, shrugging us off its back so we fell squarely and sorely on our bottoms.

The postman looked up in surprise. We jumped up and crowded together to block the alley where the tiger skin rug had parked itself. The postman, unlike the railway man at Waterloo, smiled kindly. His voice was nasal and clownish as if he were wearing a red rubber nose.

"Hello there. Are you alright? You look lost."

"Eh, no, thank you, eh, well, maybe, sorry, I mean, yes please." I took a deep breath, like Joanna had told me to do, and tried again. "We're on our way to Coventry University. We're, eh, visiting someone." The postman smiled that way grown-ups sometimes do, secretly finding something amusing.

"Ah, well, perhaps I can help you. I'm going that way myself—it's up this lane to the main road, and pretty much a straight walk west from there. Come with me and I'll set you in the right direction."

We knew the rule that you're not to talk to strangers, never go along with them anywhere. I hesitated. There was no backing out of the street, otherwise the postman might see the rug. But we couldn't go forwards either because that would be going with the postman, who, though in a tidy uniform and friendly, was still a stranger. We were stuck again.

I was waiting for the tiger to do something, willing it to do something, even disappear, so we could get out of this pickle, but the tiger did nothing. The postman stepped closer and I didn't like him doing that, even though he was trying to be helpful. Why couldn't Baba screech up now in his big red car and hoot its horn? Why couldn't we be back in Granny's kitchen eating pancakes and listening to stories? Why did we have to be here, trapped down a narrow street?

"Don't be scared," said the postman, "I don't bite. But I tell you what, I'll give the community police officer a call. Lost children belong with police, not posties," and he pulled a phone from his pocket. Jenny started poking me on the back.

"Do something. Do something, Lal."

But I didn't know what to do. I knew how to sort a Rubik's Cube, I could recite huge chunks of the Bhagavad Gita—a gigantic Hindu verse—and I'd recently hit the topmost level on my new computer game. But right now, I didn't know how to stop the postman calling the police.

The postman was dithering and muttering about poor phone reception. I turned to the others for help. Jenny had taken a few steps backwards to hide Dilip, who'd retreated into the alley and was crouching low— and whispering to the rug.

This time, his whispers were faster than usual, and almost visible, little droplets floating and hanging in the air. The sound gathered into a soft mist. Dilip kept on whispering. Drifting past and around us, the mist filled the alleyway and seeped out into the small street, making us shiver. Soon we were wrapped in the white haze and could hardly see the postman, who had moved away a little to make his call to the police. Time was running out. But now he turned in surprise.

"Are you all right there, kids? Oi, are you OK?" His voice trailed away as the mist thickened. He stood on tiptoes to see us above it, but in seconds it had gathered as thick as candy floss and completely masked us. Dilip was waving wildly for us to sit on the rug. As soon as we did, the rug lifted up.

The mist was cold. The postman was still calling out, but I could barely hear him. I wanted to shout back, tell him we were OK, thank him, but I couldn't find the right words. Like with Joanna at the gallery, I felt a stab of guilt—the postman would be left wondering what on earth had just happened.

The rug wavered before swiftly and silently speeding to the end of the street. It turned west at the main road, as the postman had said to, and, draped in fog, veered through the morning traffic.

The fog had caused all sorts of commotion on the streets. Enough to allow the tiger to take us unseen to a quiet road at the delivery entrance to the university. Behind the gates were the big blocks of brick and small squares of glass of the campus buildings. The rug landed gently and when we climbed down, it morphed again into the tiger. The mist hung low and drifted with us as we walked.

On a large board map, we found the Department of Conservation and Biodiversity. That sounded right. The tiger had come a little way with us, leaning low into what was left of the cover, but now it dipped into an empty lecture room. The university was quiet. When we reached the department, we found the reception closed.

"Can I help?" A university porter in overalls approached. He looked Indian, but his accent was from square in the middle of England. I told him we were looking for Professor Chatterjee and the man replied, "Oh, yes, I know Chatterjee. But you're out of luck. He's away at a conference. India. He'll be back on campus in a week or so. There's a notice on his office door, Room 121," and he pointed into the building.

"Thanks!" I said and noted the name on his lanyard, Sami.

The professor's door was a noticeboard of post-its, postcards, lists and sign-up sheets. Pinned in the centre was the note.

I am on research leave and attending the International Conservation Conference, Institute of Technology, Mumbai, India.

"Oh, no!" cried Jenny. "It's dated Thursday—that's already two days ago."

"And it doesn't say when he'll be back," added Dilip. According to Sami, it wouldn't be any time soon.

"Let's fetch the tiger," I sighed.

In the empty lecture hall, we hunched down with the big cat.

"What now? Do we have to go back to Greystanes?" Dilip asked.

Jenny shook her head sternly, mouth full of a caramel wafer. She'd shared out a few more, keeping the last pack back for an emergency. The wafer was powdery, making me hungry for one of Naniji's syrupy snacks. I glanced at the ring on Jenny's finger.

"Yeah, I think we have to go back to Scotland," I replied. "We can post the ring to the Professor's office."

"But he won't be back from India for *weeks*!" Jenny spat bits of wafer out and her eyes filled up with tears. She swallowed hard. "What about the tiger's promise? And what if your mum and dad get rid of the rug before the professor gets back and gets his message? And what if the snake man is still after us?"

We sat bickering about what to do. The tiger was restless. I watched its swaying stripes as it paced behind the podium. The mission was about so much more than a few promises now. Jenny was right, we couldn't wait any longer. The tiger seemed to reach the same conclusion at the same time as me—I felt prickles in my fingertips and reached out to touch it. We both knew that the other understood. It was the closest I'd come to understanding how Dilip and the tiger spoke. The tiger lowered itself next to me.

"Come, let's go," I said to the others, standing up, dusting down and helping them on to the tiger's back. Jenny was fizzing; Dilip's lower lip was wobbling.

"Where are we going to, Lal?" he asked as he scooted up to make space for me. I pulled myself on to the tiger and patted it gently on the hind. As I wrapped my arms round Dilip, I was filled with a sense of total responsibility. Or maybe it was dread. We held tight as the tiger slunk from the hall and bounded forwards and upwards into a sky of slow-drifting clouds. "Lal, where are we going?" Dilip repeated.

"To find Professor Chatterjee," I called forwards. "To India. Where else?"

15

IN THE GUTTER

A thin peel of yellow light marked the horizon, but it was still dark when we arrived. The journey was cold and, like dreams, stretched for hours but was over in seconds. This time, the landing was like no other. The tiger threw itself down heavily, its strong legs coming to life, folding back and rebounding so that when we hit the ground, we hit it running. Dewy air washed our faces as the tiger, back legs in unison and front paws punching forwards one after the other, bounded through the wide streets. Thrown forwards, we drew our knees inwards.

Although the light was low, people were about. The floodlit façade of a bank and a colourful strip of shops glossed by. The tiger darted into darkness. Still at pace, it kept to the shadows, but someone had spotted us. A voice called out from an apartment window, a torch beamed, and the tiger flexed up and over a high wall.

It was a close call. The shouting died down; the torch

went out. The tiger slowed to a stop, moved its head from side to side and sniffed the air. My heart was still sprinting.

"Lal?" Dilip leaned back. "Lal, where are we now?"

I patted him briskly on the leg and could hardly believe my own words.

"India, my boy," and I sounded like an echo of Baba. I shook off the thought—Baba was so far away, too far away, now. Dilip pinched me in disbelief. At last, we were back in India. I looked to Jenny proudly and was startled by the look of disgust on her face.

We were in India, but not the India we'd been boasting about, not the India we'd been missing. The tiger had landed in a squalid corner off a dirt-track side street. Litter and scrap-piles surrounded us. The rushing cold air had smelled of nothing, but now that we'd stopped, our nostrils filled with the stench of rot and waste. Jenny clapped a hand over her mouth, gagging. I dipped my eyes away from her. We hadn't told her about this side of India—its poor side.

The tiger paused, its ears flat back.

There was a murmur as a small crowd turned into the nearby side road. The tiger backed up and hunched into a ditch, jolting us backwards and then forwards into each other. The crowd passed, but the tiger remained still and tense; it took me a moment in the dawn light to see why. We were face-to-face with of a huddle of children, curled into a concrete drainpipe. The tiger's tail flicked, its head lowering at the threat. I gently patted its hind.

"Hi. *Namaste,*" I said. The children in the circular pipe stared over, eyes like Indian bush babies, large and round.

Out of the darkness, a small voice replied, "Hi," and, "*Kay apne sher chora hai?*" which means, "Have you stolen a tiger?"

"*Nahin!* No!" I smiled and continued in Hindi, "But don't worry, it won't hurt you." The girl who'd spoken wriggled her way out of the tangle of bodies in the drain and stood with clenched fists on her hips.

"I know it won't hurt me," she said defiantly. "I'm not scared. I fight all sorts. A tiger is nothing."

The tiger hauled itself to standing. The street urchin had long dark hair, looping in two thick, long braids to her ears. Her clothes were filthy, and her skin was yellowish with dirt and disease. The beady eyes of the others went on staring. I slipped down off the tiger's back.

"*Mera nama Lal hai,*" I spoke in Hindi—my name is Lal. "What's your name?"

"Who wants to know?" said the girl, and added quickly, "It's Mani."

"Mani," I repeated. It meant jewel, gemstone. Her eyes sparkled dangerously. "We need help. Can you help us? Please?"

"What kind of help?"

"We need to get to the Institute of Technology. I don't have a map. And we can't be seen. We need to go by back streets, so we won't get caught. Can you help us?"

Mani smirked. "I don't need a map. I know every back street."

I doubted this. Mumbai was a megacity sprawling over six hundred square kilometres, dense with twenty million people plus. But, if she thought she could help... I was halfway through thanking her when she cut in.

"What's it worth?"

I'd forgotten this bit, forgotten that everything on India's streets, even help, had to be paid for, haggled over. A riddle wouldn't work here. I looked at Jenny's finger, but the gold ring wasn't there. She must have hidden it. Mani took a step forward.

"What's it worth?" she repeated, sharpening her tone. She was more like broken glass than a shining gemstone. Slowly, the other children morphed from a darksome mess of limbs into two rakish boys and twin girls, sitting up to listen. I had no idea what to say. What could we possibly offer this street girl and her grubby gang?

"*Kya?* What do you want?" I shrugged. One of the boys kicked out idly at Mani, slurring something in a slow, muddy voice, too low for me to hear. Mani looked triumphant as she resumed her warlike stance. But before she could say anything, Jenny interrupted.

"What are you talking about, Lal? What are they saying?" She sounded exasperated; her accent sounded out of place.

"I'm asking for their help. They can take us to the Institute."

"So, what are we waiting for?"

"They want something in return," I explained, and turned back to Mani. "OK, what can we give you?" I asked. "What do you want?"

The rakish boys and twin girls stepped out from the concrete piping. Mani licked her tongue across her top teeth and smiled a hungry smile.

"Give us the tiger," she said, and the gang, like vultures, encircled me.

16

THROUGH THE TUNNEL

Seconds felt like hours. A crow, sitting on a sagging tangle of wires overhead, cawed. From up there it must have looked like a fight was about to break out. And it was.

Jenny had jumped from the tiger's back into the gutter. I'd translated to her that they wanted the tiger and that had done it: Jenny had snapped. She hurled herself into the circle and shoved at Mani. Mani pushed back and everyone stepped outwards as the two girls flew at each other. I tried to stop Jenny, but one of the boys held me back with a wiry forearm. Jenny and Mani tugged down, fists full of bright curls and dark braids.

The tiger growled a low growl and bristled, but the street kids didn't flinch—the twins even took sticks and started poking at it. The tiger coiled its body round, tail bushy, but the twins didn't stop.

"Jenny!" I shouted as she launched forwards, kicking

at their sticks. Mani snatched at one when it fell and lashed out with it. From the ground, Jenny seized a shard of metal, pointing it straight at Mani. Jenny was in such a rage, I didn't think anything was going to stop her. But the whole horrible fight was ended abruptly by the tiger. Snarling, it took a quick, firm swipe—at Jenny. She dropped the metal and clasped her arm, too shocked to cry out.

There was a long pause. Mani was bent like a cricket batsman, stick at the ready and head up, panting. The tiger eased towards Jenny and licked her arm. Nobody else moved. Jenny whimpered, although the tiger hadn't hurt her; the only real harm done was to her feelings. It nosed at her chin so that she looked up, and she dried her eyes. Some animals nip or bat at their young to teach them a lesson, I knew that. The tiger was acting like Jenny was its cub, that was all.

"Sorry," Jenny said meekly to Mani, then added, "but you can't have the tiger. Tell her, Lal. He's ours. She can't have him!"

I translated into Hindi that she couldn't have the tiger.

"It doesn't belong to you," Mani retorted. "Tigers are from India. I know that. I go to school. Do you think I'm not schooled because I sleep here?" she waved her hand vaguely at the drainpipe. I hadn't thought anything about her schooling. "I'm going to be Top Minister of the whole of India when I grow up, and I will stop tourists like you coming in and stealing from us."

I was furious. I was *not* a tourist. This was India, and I was Indian! Though right now, in this horrible gutter, I didn't feel like I belonged at all. Besides, we hadn't stolen anything—what did she mean? Did she still think we'd stolen the tiger? I had the urge to shout at her, but now she knew about the tiger, she might call for help or tell on us.

"We haven't taken anything. Please," and I put my hand up at Jenny's protests that she couldn't understand. "We're here to help someone, and to help this tiger. We need you. You know the way. But we can't give you the tiger." I added, truthfully, "My friend said it was ours, but it isn't ours. It isn't ours to give away."

We turned to the tiger. And there, on top of its back, legs down dangling, the twins were fussing over Dilip, stroking his shiny hair and the tiger's fur and giggling.

Jenny laughed, and Mani gave a rough but happy sort of cough. The two street boys were unamused.

"Oh, Dilip," said Jenny, "trust you to save us!"

I scoffed at the idea that Dilip had saved us. Though when I thought about it, Dilip was the one who had whispered for the tiger to open the butterfly box, Dilip had saved us in the alley, and now, in the backstreets of Mumbai, Dilip was making friends instead of fighting. I should probably feel proud of him, but I was just annoyed. Dilip was funny and carefree, Dilip was cute, and even the tiger had chosen Dilip.

Mani waved a hand at me. She moved her mouth into something resembling a smile.

"*Acha hai*. OK, I can help you." She signalled to the two boys and called down the twins from the tiger's back. Dilip hopped down, too.

"Thank you, Mani," I said, "we'll give you *some*thing, I promise."

Mani fired out instructions and then said, "The others must go to school. But I can take you. I will take you to the Institute." She nodded at me and I did wonder what sort of 'school' these children went to. As though reading my mind, Mani explained. "A lady teaches us in her yard. Not far away. We count and read and she tells us stories. She gives us food, too." My tummy rumbled.

"Let's go, then," I said. And, to our surprise, Mani and the other street kids clambered back into the concrete drain. Mani looked at the gathering sky.

"Come, follow!" and she disappeared into the darkness. The tiger paced forwards and sniffed into the pipe, putting up a paw as though to test it. It turned and cocked its head—it was safe.

"Let's go, quick," I said, and we climbed into the cool chamber. With no torch, and not knowing what was ahead, we stooped further inside the pipe. The tiger leapt in behind us, blocking out the light.

17

STORM AHEAD

The tunnel stank. It was black at first, but as my eyes adjusted I made out the others' bleary figures ahead. Dirty water trickled down the sides and a shallow, slimy stream ran underfoot. Clumps of earth, occasional stones and rusty nail-ends poked up from the concrete, making it tricky not to trip.

"Fast now," Mani's voice bounced off the walls. "It will rain soon. It will flood." I pushed forwards—if the pipe flooded, we would all drown in filthy water. I prodded Dilip's back to hurry him, and as my own feet picked up pace, so did my thoughts. It was *Varsha*, the wet season, when monsoon rains swept across India making it the wettest place on earth. These were the rains that fell like hammers, the rains that gathered into rivers and swept away streets. They were the rains I'd missed so much. Now, I wished over and over for Scottish drizzle.

And then I heard it. At first it sounded like a far-off

rumbling, but it grew louder. And louder. Rushing water.

"Fast, fast!" Mani's voice was all we had to go on and we ran to it. The sound of the water was rising. The tiger was at my heels, its rasping, hot breath urging me on. The flood of water would reach us any moment now, and the noise was almost upon us, thundering. I pictured a tsunami rolling up behind us. Taking Dilip's hand, I pulled him forwards with me, running as fast as I could. A glimmer appeared ahead—the end of the tunnel. We ran towards it. The light at the pipeline opening grew bigger, ragged with the street kids' silhouettes. I jumped towards them and we all poured out.

It was like being under a waterfall, water pummelling from straight above. The gushing noise wasn't from flooding pipes, but from water spilling from the gutter above and from rain overhead as it crashed down from a thick sky. In seconds we were drenched. Mani ushered us through a tall gate into a sheltered patio and bolted us in. Shivering and deafened, we huddled together, watching as the rain, like a steel-grey sheet, fell and fell and fell. The smell of rain soaked me in memories and relief all at once. Dilip's shoulders juddered. I was sure he was crying, but I wasn't sure what to do. If Mum or Baba were here, they'd scoop him up. But Mum and Baba were four thousand gigantic miles away.

Unexpectedly, Mani wiped Dilip's cheeks and flashed him a smile. She took his small hand in hers and, over the din, beckoned for us to follow her through a narrow door.

We found ourselves in a dark room, sparsely furnished and damp. Mani and the street kids took off their shoes and we did, too. We scuffed an ugly wooden cabinet to a corner, for the tiger to hide behind. Mani hastily covered it over with cloth.

She led us along a short passage. I caught up with Jenny.

"Where's the ring?"

"Safe." She patted in her jacket pocket and I gave her a double thumbs-up.

The passage opened to a bright courtyard. The rain had turned off like a tap. Metal buckets had been arranged to collect drips from the roof edges. Sunlight danced off window panes and puddles.

"Auntie! Auntie!" called Mani. A tall woman in a pale pink sari drew back the curtain of a doorway and smiled in surprise.

"Hallo, more children!" she said in English.

"These are tourists, Auntie," Mani said, sticking out her chin towards us. "They need help."

I stepped forward and told her how we urgently needed to reach someone at the Institute of Technology. Mani chipped in that she could take us. A frown of concern crossed Auntie's brow.

"I'm not sure, Mani. Tourist children travelling

alone?" She wanted to 'tell the authorities'. Why did all grown-ups want to do that? Couldn't they make up their own minds about what was right and wrong? Mani pleaded with her and Auntie softened, insisting that we come in and eat first.

She sent for our saturated shoes and wrung them out with strong hands, packed them with old newspaper and arranged them in front of a stove to help them dry quickly. She hung up our jackets and made us change into dry clothes. One of the boys gave me and Dilip some dry cotton V-necks and loose pants. When I said thanks, the boy skulked away without looking at me. Auntie took Mani and Jenny to change into salwar kameez.

The kitchen smelled of glycerine soap and sandalwood. Shiny pots and yellow onions dangled from a ceiling blackened by smoke. When Jenny reappeared, I had to do a double take. She was in a pink-and-green salwar and her hair had been brushed and braided—she didn't look like Jenny. She looked... pretty.

Auntie set out a game like snakes and ladders for us to play while she cooked. When the food was ready, we dug into creamy hot dhal and fresh roti greased with ghee. Jenny wolfed hers and gave a loud belch—she was back to being herself.

"Excuse me!" she said, covering her mouth. But Auntie tipped her head approvingly and dished Jenny more food. I smiled—in Granny's house, unlike Auntie's, burping was not a sign of appreciation.

The food was comforting, but the nutty flavours of the lentils reminded me of home cooking, and the warm round flatbread made me think of pancake stories. I wished Granny was here telling us all a story now. I scraped my plate clean and washed my fingers in water from a little enamel bowl. Auntie set out some floor cushions and ordered us to rest. We sat down but couldn't relax.

Mani spoke to Auntie in a language I didn't recognise. It sounded like Marathi, but it could have been any of India's hundreds of languages.

"OK," Mani turned to us at last. "We must go now because it will take a long time for me to take you to the Institute and come back." She slung a leather holster carrying a water bottle across her shoulder. Auntie fussed over us for a while. She gave me a canvas bag with our half-dried clothes and our jackets packed inside it (except Jenny's—she insisted on wearing hers). We said thanks and left the way we'd come in.

"OK," ordered Mani, when everyone had put on their shoes and the tiger was out of hiding. "Everybody listen. We go first by tunnel and second by rooftop. Keep close. The tiger can't be seen."

And that was it, she was off, back into the drainpipe.

Light seeped away. I tracked the sound of Mani's footsteps. They were not as fast as before. Dilip and

Jenny were splashing and tripping, the tiger behind. A rat scuttled past. We kept going, turning corners and chasing echoes, until at last we reached another opening.

Mani squatted briefly, turned and climbed on to the ridge of the jutting pipe, expertly pulling herself up the irregular bricks of the adjoining building and onto its roof. We went after her, less expertly. The tiger sprang up from the muddy ditch. By the time we were all up, Mani was ten feet ahead, flitting along the edge of the roof and ducking under strings of electric wires.

"Wait for us!" I called. The rooftops were uneven. Some were flat, others tiled; most were slanting corrugated iron, rusty in places and slippery in others. Laundry flapped from swaying pulleys, and air conditioning units belched out stale air.

"Mani, you have to slow down a bit!"

Mani slowed and we regrouped on a roof terrace above a busy bus station. The tiger lay low and we rested against it, getting our breath back.

Far to the north, storm clouds were bleeding like dark ink on thin tissue.

"Jenny, where's the ring now?" I wanted to know.

"Here," she said, unzipping the pocket of her summer jacket. She put her hand in and groped around. Her face flushed scarlet. She looked up, first at me, then at Dilip and then at the tiger. "Oh my—"

"You haven't!" I hissed at her. "Check again. You can't

have—check again."

I began checking, too, seeing if I could find the unfindable in Jenny's pockets. She desperately patted her kameez and checked her shoes. She took off her jacket so every zip and sleeve could be opened, emptied and searched. And then she let out a loud, angry sob. Thunder rumbled closer in. The tiger gave a low whine.

Jenny had lost the ring.

18

A ROOF RACK RIDE

I punched a brick chimney. My fist immediately throbbed, but I shook it out and pretended it didn't. The others hadn't noticed anyway—they were all looking down, heads low. Jenny was crying, but I didn't feel sorry for her. She'd lost the ring, lost the message for Menon Chatterjee.

Mani lifted her head. She snorted, hacked up phlegm, and spat.

"I know where it is," she said plainly, her eyes glinting. No, she doesn't, I thought. She hadn't known there was a ring in the first place.

"Where? How?" I challenged her.

"Let's say, I know someone who likes to pick things out of pockets," she replied in quick Hindi, standing up. "If something you had is stolen, I know who stole it. Let me go and get it."

"Who? From where?"

Mani gave the name of one of the two rakish boys in her gang. I might have guessed—the one that hadn't been able to look me in the eye.

"We'll come with you," I said, not entirely trusting her, and not wanting to be left behind.

"I'll be faster on my own. I can take the tiger with me." It was more of a statement than a request. "The tiger will scare him into giving me the ring."

I looked to the tiger, whose tongue was out, panting. It looked thirsty. Could a magical tiger get thirsty?

"What's happening?" asked Jenny. Neither Dilip or I answered.

"It'll take ages for you to go back," I said.

Dilip tapped my knee.

"The tiger can carry her. It will save time," he said. We both looked from the tiger to the street girl. I didn't doubt the tiger, but I did doubt Mani and wasn't sure she could be trusted with the secret of the tiger skin rug. All she knew so far was that there was a real tiger with us, like a pet. "It will save time," Dilip repeated. It did seem the best option, and the fastest way for Mani to retrieve the ring.

"What's going on?" asked Jenny again. I was still fizzing that Jenny had lost the message, even though I knew now it wasn't her fault, it had been pinched from her. While Dilip told Mani about the tiger, I filled Jenny in on what Mani had said.

"He stole the ring from me? The little… Wait till I get my hands on him!"

"Jenny, Mani can get it back, and she's going to fly with the tiger."

"But," Jenny hesitated, "we'll be alone."

"They'll come straight back," I replied, nodding to the tiger as if to say, "won't you?"

Dilip asked it to show Mani how it changed. The tiger bent its head and stretched out its front legs, shimmering as it transformed, its tail shrivelling and the light in its eyes burning out. It lay flat on a square of concrete on the rooftop terrace. Mani had stepped back a little, and Jenny, Dilip and I kept glancing to her, waiting for signs of her amazement. Mani's expression didn't change. Then the tiger began to hover and twist back to life again.

"You see?" I prompted. "It's a magical tiger."

"Yes, I see," Mani shrugged. "So, let me take it and go."

Jenny, Dilip and I were speechless. Nothing in the universe was more powerful and impressive than the tiger transforming. Jenny pulled me and Dilip to the side.

"Guys, I'm not sure about this. What if it was *Mani* that—" she paused as the tiger skin rug zoomed past us, across the rooftops, Mani bent like a jockey on its back, "—took the ring," she finished as they flew out of sight.

"What do you mean, if Mani took it?" asked Dilip.

"Well, what if she was the one who pick-pocketed

from me?" Jenny's voice was rising. "And now we don't have the ring or the tiger, and we don't even know where we are," and she stamped her foot on the roof and let out another wail.

"No," Dilip sat down next to her, hugging his knees into his chest. "The tiger wouldn't leave us. It wouldn't have just left us here."

"No," I said, trying to sound like I was sure. In truth, I wasn't sure at all.

I became aware of the world around us, of rumbling engines in the bus park below. I crawled to the edge. Red and orange buses chucked out dirty fumes. Vendors selling everything from sunglasses to umbrellas, boiled eggs to blue-tailed cockerels weaved through crowds of city travellers. I returned to report what I'd seen. The sun burst out and there wasn't much shade up there on the top of the building. Mani had the water, too. How long would she and the tiger take to return? And what if they didn't?

Against the pewter-grey sky, white lightning forked. Dilip counted out the seconds until hearing the low roll of thunder. Twenty. We taught Jenny the sum and worked out that the storm was 6.6 kilometres away. My heart-rate was going up with the air pressure. Jenny wasn't crying anymore but her breathing was juddery.

"Sorry," she said.

"It's not your fault."

A hot breeze blew in and suddenly Dilip got up, standing on a chimney.

"Sit down, you'll be seen!" Jenny said, sniffing.

"Or struck by lightning," I hissed. But Dilip didn't seem to hear us. I followed his gaze, and out from behind a flapping bed-sheet, roofs away, the tiger skin rug was zooming back towards us, Mani crouched low on its top. Seconds later, they had landed, the tiger's paws pounding heavily down.

Mani climbed off the tiger's back. She brushed back a wiry strand of her black hair and held out her hand, letting the ring drop into my palm.

"You got it! I can't believe—"

"That I didn't keep it for myself?" she snorted.

"No," I shook my head. "I didn't mean—"

"I don't care," she waved, "but you should have seen his face," and a wicked grin spread across hers. She licked her chapped lips in glee. "He saw the shadow of the flying tiger, and he turned around and..." she started laughing so hard, she could hardly get the words out, "and he didn't know where to run, so..." she grunted, "he ran in circles," and she was bent double laughing.

It was impossible not to join her. Jenny was laughing, too, even though it was mostly all in Hindi.

"You should have seen him," Mani wiped her eyes,

"like a puppy chasing its tail. I had to grab him to stop him falling over. He knew what I'd come for. What *we'd* come for," she added, stepping towards the tiger to stroke its shoulder.

"Well, thanks," I said and then held out the ring to Jenny.

"What? Me? But I was the one who—"

"It fits you best. Just don't, well…"

"Lose it again? Never," she smiled.

"Come on, we have to keep going."

We lay on our tummies at the edge of the roof. Directly below was the roof-rack of a bus, bundled with trunks, suitcases and boxes.

"Where do we go now?"

"We go for a ride!" Mani smiled and jumped on to the bus. One by one, like lemmings, we jumped after her. We shifted luggage to mask the tiger. Mani sat down next to it and put her arm on its back; Jenny nestled in and stroked it possessively.

The sun was high and the station was baking hot. The bus juddered and at last started to move. I felt it in my tummy when the bus steered around a corner and gathered speed. Mani unscrewed the top of her water canister and passed it round. She pulled the salwar scarf over Jenny's head to keep her cool and Jenny managed to smile back.

At first the bus spluttered and stalled through narrow

streets, but in no time, it was speeding along a wide, smooth highway. All around, traffic throbbed. Dilip rested his head on Jenny's shoulder and closed his eyes, but Jenny craned her neck over the cases and boxes.

"I wish Granny could see this," she said.

Granny. This was like one of her stories. Magical tigers, street urchins, a faraway city…

After a long time, the bus slowed to a chug. The roofs in this station were all super high, too high to jump onto or clamber up. The station assistants would soon begin to haul down luggage. There was nowhere to hide, or to hide the tiger.

Luckily, Mani had an idea. As the passengers tumbled out, she stood on a box and wolf-whistled. With her hands clasped outwards, she began pleading with passengers and station assistants to let her hand down bags from the rooftop in exchange for a small number of rupees. The assistants started shouting, "Get down!" and, "Stop begging!"

Some passengers shouted that they should help the orphan, but most were against it. The crowd was so focused on her that they didn't notice Dilip and the tiger sliding down the other side of the bus and disappearing underneath it. Neither did I at first.

"Follow the tiger!" Mani ordered me and Jenny, as she threw someone his holdall and caught the coin tossed in return. Jenny and I clambered down the side of the bus and joined Dilip and the tiger in the dirty shade of the undercarriage. Porters and assistants were getting angry.

"Hey, urchin, stop stealing our tips!" they yelled. We heard the driver step off the bus and demand Mani go. Soon, she was crouching next to me.

"Now what?"

"Now, we run," and she sprang from the belly of the bus to the shade of a food cart, and from there to a thin gap between two buildings. We sprinted after her, not daring to look back. The tiger must have been quick as a flash—no one seemed to notice us. It was a tight squeeze in the passageway, but out at the other side we found ourselves at the edge of an enormous city park. All around the fringes were trees and shrubs, thick and lush from monsoon rains.

From inside the bushes, I could see a cricket match. I loved playing cricket in big park spaces, knowing that Baba was in the crowd tallying up scores and cheering me on. Ajay and I would scoff vanilla cones after a match, not caring that the heat had turned the ice-cream sour as lemons. I peered through the foliage. Distant voices rose and fell, there was occasional applause and the *puck* of bat against ball. I was in India but Ajay was as far away as ever. I turned away from the figures in whites.

Ahead, big bushes and shrubs ran to the banks of a large lake. The tiger crept through the undergrowth to the water-edge and began lapping soundlessly. I wondered if it was really drinking, or if it didn't need to eat and drink, like Dilip had said.

"Water?" Mani handed around her canister again.

"How far do we have to go?" Jenny asked.

Mani pointed. "We're nearly there. See that pylon over there? That's part of the Institute."

"Really?" I almost choked. In no more than minutes we would be there. "Then let's keep going."

We had to be careful in places where the wooded parts of the city park ran alongside the road or came too close to play areas. Mani stopped abruptly.

"OK. I leave you here. You can see the gates of the Institute." She pointed through the greenery to a large entrance with a steel boom that went up and down when cars went in or out.

I didn't want Mani to leave us.

"You promised we'd give her something," Dilip whispered.

I nodded and looked at her—dusty, unpredictable. It felt like she'd been with us the whole adventure, but we'd only met at sunrise. Mani smiled, showing gaps between her brown teeth. She gently touched the tiger's shiny back. The tiger pawed at the air, twisting its head around and yawning out a low, circular sound.

"He's saying thank you," said Dilip.

I unstrapped my watch and had only started to present it to Mani when she snatched it out of my hand.

"And these!" offered Jenny—the remaining, bashed-up packet of caramel wafers from her coat pocket. Mani was delighted and squirrelled them into her clothes. We said an awkward goodbye. Mani turned and, her hands together in thanks, bowed to the tiger. Before any of us could say anything else, she'd cut through the bushes and was gone.

19

UNDER THE PIPAL TREE

We were alone, the three of us and the tiger. The gates to the Institute loomed. Guards were checking passes and inspecting vehicles. There was no way we could slip in with a tiger without being seen.

Jenny offered to stay behind. She and the tiger would be safe and camouflaged in the greenery and flower bushes.

"Besides, I'd stick out like a sore thumb," she said. "All freckly with frizzy hair. But you might need this," and she gave me the gold ring.

I walked ahead of Dilip, who was balancing his way along the black-and-white painted kerb. At the gates to the Institute my voice didn't waver once when I asked to be put in the direction of the 'International Conservation Conference'. The guard asked who we were, and a second one strode across to jeer at our outfits, which were filthy again.

"We're looking for our uncle," I told him.

"Well, when you find him, tell him to buy you some clean kurtas, hey!" and the guards laughed and pointed the way. We tried not to draw attention to ourselves by rushing. A conference poster showed the way to the quadrangle. Following a narrow path marked out with a neat box hedge, we arrived at a courtyard dotted with trees. A cleaner was mopping the shaded walkway and when we asked where the conference was, he pointed to the far corner. The door to the conference room was closed, but I could see a roomful of people through the louvre windows. The cleaner had followed us round, curious.

"They'll be out soon," he said. "They're going to break for lunch. Lunch is in the venue next door." I nodded in thanks and peeked into the room again. At the front table, five people sat perspiring behind microphones. In front of each speaker was a small placard, and the one in the middle read, 'Professor Chatterjee, Coventry University, U.K.'

I looked from the placard to the professor. He was thinner and his beard was whiter than his website profile picture, but it was definitely the same person.

"Don't freak out," I said to Dilip in a slightly freaked-out voice, "but Menon Chatterjee is in that room."

The earlier monsoon storm we'd seen from the rooftops had drifted away. In place of stale street smells were the scents of freshly drenched grass and wet concrete, which faded as the day grew hotter. The conference party was running late for lunch. We waited in the quadrangle under the shade of a pipal tree, leaning on its raised roots. A battalion of fat black ants marched by. The air grew heavy; waiting grew boring. Dilip sketched with a thin stick in the earth. I leaned back against the smooth grey bark of the trunk and closed my eyes.

In Indian stories, the pipal tree was where the gods met, and things were decided. Maybe the cool shade of the pipal was simply a good place to think clearly. I half opened my eyes—the cleaner was in a store cupboard next to us, restocking his trolley. The cupboard opened out onto a covered walkway. Straining against the sun, I tried to see what else was in the small room. The cleaner moved off, leaving the door unlocked. By the time the conference room door opened, and a chattering stream of academics were spilling out for their lunch, I had a plan.

"OK, Dilip, stay here," I said, pulling myself up. "I'm going over to that cupboard. Keep watch and keep quiet. I'm going to find the professor," and I didn't wait for him to reply. A few minutes later, dressed in starched white waiter's clothes, I reappeared from the storeroom and winked past Dilip to the lunch hall.

Slipping behind one of the buffet tables, I took up my pose as a server. The vats of rice, cauldrons of steaming curries and platters of warm breads made my mouth water. I saw Professor Chatterjee joining the queue, tailed by a group of eager students.

"Sir," I said, when he reached me, putting a heavy dollop of dhal on his plate, "I have a message from your mother." The professor looked startled.

"Are you talking to me?" he asked. I nodded. "Well, I'm afraid you are mistaken." He tried to move on but the queue ahead of him had slowed to a jam.

"We looked for you in Coventry, sir, but the porter—um, Sami—told us you were here." The professor looked baffled as I went on. "We came with this message, sir. Here," and I reached out to the professor. He opened his hand and I pressed the ring gently into it. The professor looked down at the golden band in his palm, his cheeks darkening. He rolled it round and squinted down at the engraving. He stared at me, standing there in my oversized clothes serving dhal.

"Who are you?"

But the line for lunch had started to move again. I was kept busy with the next plate, and the next.

"Meet me at the pipal tree in the quadrangle," I called after him as the lunch queue progressed, the hall filled, and the professor was jostled and bustled out of sight.

Lunch service took ages. Afterwards, wiping my

brow on my sleeve, I stepped into the sunshine not quite believing what had happened. I changed quickly. I couldn't wait to tell Dilip—I'd spoken to the professor, I'd given him the ring! The tiger's promise had been kept. The weight on my shoulders began inching off.

Dilip was standing on a tree root like a meerkat. He hopped down when he saw me, and I knew at once that something was wrong.

"He was here, Lal," and Dilip looked terrified. "The man in the snake jacket. He showed up in the middle of lunch. I had to hide behind the tree. He paid the cleaner to tell him what hotel Menon Chatterjee is staying in," said Dilip, shaking. I pulled Dilip back behind the wide trunk of the tree. I was confused. Had the man been after Menon Chatterjee, not us, all along? He wanted the tiger skin rug, we knew that much. Maybe he was also trying to get the message to Menon... or to stop him getting the message.

"Good work, Dilip," I said, trying to hide that I was terrified, too.

When lunch was over, the delegates plodded back to the meeting room, Professor Chatterjee among them. At the last moment, though, the professor side-stepped away from the others and towards the pipal tree. Dilip's worries seem to evaporate when he saw the professor. He beamed round the trunk at him.

"Who *are* you?" demanded the professor. "What do you want from me? And what does this mean?" he asked, holding up the ring.

"It's a message from your mother."

"No, it's not," replied the professor evenly. "I want to know where you got this ring and why you are giving it to me."

This was not the response we'd expected. The professor seemed angry, and the message seemed only half-delivered. The tiger wouldn't be able to rest, surely, if the message hadn't been understood.

"Well?" insisted the professor.

"Let's take him to the tiger, Lal?" Dilip suggested.

"What was that?" the professor asked.

Dilip was right, there wasn't any other way of explaining ourselves in a way that the professor would believe.

"There's someone you need to meet," I said and began walking from the quadrangle out to the city park.

20

TRAVELLING ALONE

The professor was in a state of shock. It seemed he couldn't quite comprehend that he was sitting cross-legged in a thicket of waxy leaves and creepers, with two boys, a girl from Scotland, and a very large and very present tiger. He turned the ring over and over in his fingers. Eventually, he looked up.

"Right. OK. But I don't quite get it all. Your tiger, which I admit is clearly not an ordinary tiger, otherwise it would not be keeping us company so nicely," he muttered almost to himself, setting out everything we'd told him, "—this tiger of yours is most of the time a rug. And it talks, it talks somehow. Let me get this right. It told you—Dilip, a small boy—that it had a promise to keep. So, you two brothers and this friend Jenny, yes, Jenny, who lives with her grandmother and is an orphan, correct? The three of you decided to help it. But there is a man in a snake jacket, of all things, and he also wants the tiger, or this ring, or maybe just me. He followed you to London, you think, where you had *flown* on the back of the tiger," and he cleared his throat before going on.

"In London, you acquired this ring in exchange for a riddle. You tracked me down—Lal, who is the oldest, found my details on some sort of website, correct? To give it to me, you flew, again on the aforementioned tiger, to Coventry. A porter, Sami in fact—yes, I know Sami—told you I was here, in India. You decided that instead of posting the ring to my pigeon-hole, you would all come here to give the ring to me in person. So, you came to India—again," he swallowed hard, "flying on the back of this very tiger." He looked at the cat, and from the cat to us. "Correct?"

Nobody responded. It was, after all, exactly what had happened. It did sound a bit crazy. I was sort of caught between two worlds. I knew that everything was true, even the magic. I also knew that in the world of adults and reason and science and fact, none of it (especially the magic) could be happening.

"So, forgetting *what* and *how*, the thing I don't quite get," the professor continued, "is *why*? Why are you doing this?" He looked each of us in the eyes. Quickly thinking of what the professor might want to hear, I volunteered a reason.

"The tiger was poached, you know, and we thought our parents might get in trouble for trying to sell an illegal tiger rug."

The others nodded. "And the tiger needs help," Dilip said, "and Lal said to help it."

"It couldn't rest until it kept its promise," Jenny added.

The professor rubbed his eyes and then his beard. He studied the tiger, which was cleaning its claws and occasionally batting its tail. "Well, it has kept its promise now," he said, "so why isn't it, er... resting?"

I answered as tactfully as I could. "Maybe because you didn't seem to get the message?"

"And it has another promise to keep," explained Dilip. "It's going to take us home."

"I see," the professor rubbed his eyes and beard again. "Well, I don't know what to make of it all." He was talking to himself again. "I suppose I must go along with it." He lay his hands flatly on his knees and lifted his voice. "Well, I'm very grateful. The ring was given to me by my mother, but she died when I was quite young. My father was keeping the ring safe for me."

"Oh, so the message is actually from your father?" asked Jenny.

"Yes, I believe so. We had a great quarrel, decades ago. I left home, went to England and I'm completely ashamed to say that I have never been back. I sent letters, of course, but," he faltered, "they were not answered. But I think this ring was my father's way of asking me to return."

Warm wind blew in off the playing fields and rattled the foliage.

"Right," said the professor, "we'd better get you kids back safely."

"Don't worry, the tiger will do that," smiled Dilip, who was sitting as close to the professor as he could get. "After he has been back to the forest. He wants to go back. He'll meet us at your father's house."

"What?" Jenny and I gawped at Dilip.

"The tiger—" Dilip started.

"Oh yes, 'The tiger said'!" I imitated Dilip's know-it-all voice. "Dilip," I sighed, "we can't go with the professor. Mum and Baba will be worrying."

"Worrying?" moaned Jenny. "I'm dead—Granny'll shoot me," and then she winced apologetically at the tiger.

"It's not up to me," said Dilip. "The tiger said so."

I was rolling my eyes again when the tiger decided to join in the conversation. Muzzle closed, it dropped its chin into its paws and started to whimper. Not a disgruntled cat noise; more like a lonely dog. We didn't need Dilip to translate—the tiger was pleading.

"Aw," Jenny hugged it and looked at me accusingly. I started to protest but everyone else was agreeing that we should make our way to the professor's father's house, which turned out to be at the top of a mountain surrounded by forest. The tiger intended to travel to the forest on its own. To get there, the rest of us would take a train northwards out of the city and from there walk to a tea plantation where the professor knew a lodge we could stay at for the night. After that, we could take a cab up the mountain road—but the tiger must make its own way there.

"It's far too risky taking it with us on this stretch of the journey," the professor insisted, saying we would all be safest if we travelled separately. The tiger didn't object, but we did. None of us wanted to part with the tiger in the city park. It pressed its tawny forehead against each of us and I stroked its big face. Separating was difficult— Dilip had to be dragged out of the bushes.

At a wide intersection, the professor hailed a motor rickshaw, a three-wheeled taxi, and we piled in, sharing a bench and holding on as it hurtled into the carousel of vehicles on the roundabout and out towards the railway station. With honking horns, revving mopeds, and buses churning out brown filth, we were back in the familiar hustle and thrum of Indian traffic. But squashed between me and the professor, Jenny was turning a peculiar shade of green. The roads where she'd always lived were quiet, wide and orderly.

"It's OK, not far now, I can see a train up ahead," I said as we lurched forwards at a junction.

"I feel sick," Jenny said grimly. The professor shouted at the driver and the rickshaw jolted to a stop at the edge of the road. We all climbed out. Professor Chatterjee smiled at Jenny.

"A bit of a change for you, all this, hey? Well, it's quicker to walk from here anyway." We followed him and stopped at a pop-up market to buy a backpack. The professor also bought us all hats. A woman with a cool-box strapped to her bicycle tried to sell us clear plastic bags filled with frozen juice. "No, no," warned Chatterjee, "the water might not be boiled clean, I don't want you catching bugs!" and he steered us away. People stared at Jenny, and when some started tugging on her, the professor made her walk between us like we were her bodyguards.

The train station was nothing like the ones in England, not even the Underground. Hundreds and hundreds of people crowded on platforms and swarmed in and out of train doors and train windows. One man passed us pulling a goat by a rope into a carriage, and another swung a long horizontal pole with dried fish dangling off it above everyone's heads. Music weaved through the people, different kinds of music clashing together from different corners of the station. Jenny held my hand tightly as the professor led us to the high steps of a huge diesel engine.

We found empty benches in a First Class booth. The professor closed the door. It wasn't long before a ticket man popped his head in, and then a man pushing a food trolley. Bottled water and tubs of spiced vegetable rice were dished round. Soon, the train puckered and rolled out of the station. Slowly, ever so slowly, it wound its way out of the city. A conductor came by and checked our tickets and offered us cotton sheets.

Jenny yawned.

"Can we have a nap?" asked Dilip. I thought back to Greystanes when Naniji went for her nap and Dilip magicked up the tiger.

"Lal, can you help?" the professor was lowering down bunks from the walls of the booth. He stayed sitting on the lower bench and we climbed up and curled onto plastic-coated mattresses.

I closed my eyes to the steady rocking of the carriage. Despite the slow pace of the train, my mind was racing. Where was the tiger? Would it fly? Without Dilip, could it? Where was the man in the snake jacket—who was he? Why was he tracking down the professor?

I climbed down from my bunk. The professor was sitting up, gazing out to fields of whisky yellow. I sat opposite him at Dilip's feet and looked out, too.

"Still a couple of hours to go," noted the professor. "You can go back to sleep if you wish. Our stop is the end of the line, so we won't miss it."

"I wasn't sleeping."

"Oh, something on your mind?"

"It's, well…" I wasn't sure I should say anything.

"Professor, the tiger said that, 'Time would take care of itself', but time is ticking on and on and we're travelling further and further away. From Mum and Baba, I mean."

The professor leaned down on his arms and closed his eyes briefly to the billowing air.

"I think we should trust the tiger, Lal. It's taken you this far. The tiger will get you back safe. But if anything should go wrong, I should probably know something more about you. What's your surname?"

"Patel."

The professor smiled.

"Patel. A good name. Do you know what it means?" and I didn't. "It means 'village headman'. Patels are good leaders, Lal, in the old ways of thinking. I think this is true of you, isn't it? You've taken the lead in this expedition, haven't you?"

I hadn't really thought of it that way, me as leader. Jenny was the bossiest. And Dilip had the powers that brought the tiger to life, the one who could talk its ancient language. But Dilip didn't really decide things much. I *was* the oldest (apart from the tiger). Being oldest meant being the responsible one, even if you didn't want to be. It was the tiger who'd led us here, though, so maybe the tiger was our leader.

The tiger. What if it didn't make it back to the mountain forest?

The ring on the professor's finger sparkled.

"What do you think the man in the snake jacket wants?" I asked.

"Well, I've been thinking about that," the professor pursed his lips. "You overheard your parents saying this person wanted the tiger skin rug. Perhaps this man knows it's magic. Can you imagine how much a magical tiger is worth?"

I hadn't thought of that, that the man in the snake jacket might see the rug as money-making. "The woman at the beauty place, Angela—she said a man had visited Ecks years ago. Someone from India. He'd asked about the tiger and the box."

"Is that so?" the professor frowned. "If it's the same person, he hasn't given up, has he? He must have a strong reason for wanting it."

"But why not just buy it from Mum and Baba like he was going to? Why follow us to London?"

The professor fiddled with his ring. "I wonder if he *was* following you, Lal. It could be co-incidence—after all, if you are both after the same thing—that is, the message and me—then you would end up in the same places."

I thought back to the day we'd spied on the snake-jacket man from Treehouse Corner. He'd spoken to Mum and then left without the rug. They might have decided not to sell it after all.

I looked out to the fields again, and to silver-blue

mountains. Something else was bothering me. It had been relatively easy (OK, not *easy*, but not impossible) for three kids to find the professor. His own father, though, hadn't managed to find him in all those years. If he'd gone to the trouble of getting a magical tiger to take his son a message, it was odd that he hadn't kept on searching when the message obviously hadn't been delivered.

The station at the end of the line was small and calm, at least in comparison to the last one. The professor waved away offers of taxi rides and hotel accommodation. He stopped to buy bottled water and a bunch of bananas, bundling them with our hats into his bag. We didn't talk much on the walk to the tea plantation.

Heat and insects strummed in the late afternoon haze. At a rise in the road, I saw the lodge ahead, a whitewashed house with a red roof. The greeting that the professor received from the lodge owners was like a long-lost brother returning.

After a simple supper, we got a bucket of clean water each to wash with. Not long after sundown, the lodge owner gave us clean bedclothes and showed us to our rooms—one for us and one for the professor.

We climbed into our beds. We showed Jenny how to tuck her net into her mattress, so she'd be safe from mosquitoes. She said it made her feel like a princess, but my net had big holes in it, making me feel like a pauper.

"I can't sleep," Dilip whispered before he'd even tried.

"Me neither," whispered Jenny. "What about the tiger? When will we see it again?"

None of us knew. As we lay in the dark, I started telling the story of Rashiecoats. We were all asleep before she'd even run away.

21

THE LEGEND OF THE FOREST GODDESS

I buried my head under the pillow to block out the cockerel. The sun wasn't up yet. The cockerel crowed again—Granny was right, I thought sleepily, it turned out there *was* a cockerel around Greystanes. And then I remembered, we weren't at Greystanes, weren't in Scotland. We were in India. On a sloping hill at the foot of a mountain. With Menon Chatterjee. Without the tiger.

I threw the pillow off and sat up inside my netted bed. Dilip was sprawled out and snoring. Jenny was soundless. There was a chill in the air. I lay back and yanked my blanket up to my chin, staying still until the tea plantation bell clanged, calling pickers to the fields. I got up.

It was a whole hour before the others emerged, by which time I'd eaten boiled eggs and roti with the workers and dressed back into my fresh pyjama top and jogging pants, my only clean clothes. I'd walked to the tea plantation and watched sari-clad women, some carrying babies, pick and cast leaves into baskets on their hips or heads. It looked like hard work, even in the kind, pink light of morning.

When I saw the others, they looked fresher than I felt, and I envied their longer sleep. Jenny was jumping to get going.

"Let's not keep the tiger waiting!"

But the professor and our host had some bad news.

"It appears the road is out of commission," the professor announced. The lodge owner was wringing her hands, muttering that the road was "unmotorable".

"Don't worry," the professor sounded hopeful. "The road may be unmotorable, but the mountain path is still walkable. We'll trek. We'll be there by nightfall."

"That's a serious long-cut," said the lodge owner.

Jenny groaned up at the mountain and I shared her pain. Trek? To the top? In pyjamas? But the professor insisted. We were escorted to the road in a fluster of blessings and well-wishes.

Walking started off fun. We chatted and played 'I Spy'. A single ox-drawn cart passed us on the dusty track, followed some time later by dawdling school kids. The air smelled of woodsmoke. We didn't notice at first how the path was gradually sloping upwards. The sun was warm on our backs, its rays tingling our necks, and

Jenny especially was really pleased we had hats. Our chatting tapered, strides became plods, but we kept on going, pausing only for a swig of water now and then.

The professor veered onto a thin path off the main track. It was steep and rocky. After a while, just when I was thinking my feet might fall off, the professor stopped.

"Time for a pit stop!" he announced as he led us into a cool cave. We ate, drank, and rested. "It's nearly high noon. We'll soon be in the shadow of the mountain."

Jenny was jumpy to get going, but the professor insisted we stay until the peak afternoon heat had passed. The valley stretched out green and peaceful all around. Far off, there was a tinkling of bells. Leaning against the rock, my eyelids grew heavy. The tinkling reminded me of a door opening, but I couldn't remember which door...

When I stirred awake, the professor was smiling down at me.

"Time to press on, Lal."

It hadn't been a long nap, but it was deep and refreshing—though I still wished I could take my feet off and put new ones on. Below us, the green forest rolled away for miles and miles. From somewhere in it I heard the tinkling of bells again. I followed the sound and pointed to a ring of birds circling above a stony outcrop.

"Unusual," the professor frowned. "Vultures. *Gyps indicus,* to be precise, an endangered Indian variety. Probably found some fresh carrion."

Endangered creatures, a dead animal...

"What if it's the tiger?" Jenny blurted out. We shifted uneasily at the thought.

"Can the tiger die twice?" Dilip asked.

Nobody replied. "Right, young master," the professor nodded at me, "please lead the way!"

Picking my way up the path, I had my eye on a spot up ahead—a rock that glinted like silver. It looked like another good resting place and was more than halfway to the top. The top was still hours away and I wanted this expedition over with.

I was fitter than I'd thought. Not as fit as the street kids, for sure, but I'd always been a good cricketer, and you need to be strong for that. Dilip was the climber, though—I never imagined I'd be leading him in scrambling up a mountain. If Baba saw me now, he'd ruffle my hair and I wouldn't complain.

I pushed the picture of Baba out my mind and started counting to help time pass—my steps, white stones, small orange butterflies that suddenly appeared and swiftly went. I checked round on the others. Dilip was falling behind.

"Okay!" I called, and my voice bounced back

powerfully from the hills below. "Let's stop now, for a drink." We sipped from our water canisters, heart-rates falling.

"I know this path," said the professor, "the next resting place isn't far now."

"Is that it there?" I pointed to the shining rock.

"That's it," he nodded. "It shines for a reason. Let's get there and I'll show you," and he handed me his backpack. He swung Dilip onto his back like the women on the tea plantation had done with their babies, and we set off again, up the steep path.

Cold air gusted on our hot faces as we plodded on. At last, the path levelled out to a shelf of flat, grassy ground.

"Woah!" Jenny ran forwards to the rock face. Dilip jumped from the professor's back. I dropped the bag, my muscles aching and ears hissing, and rushed to the wall of white marble, touching my cheek against its cool surface. Curving westward, part of the rock caught the afternoon light and reflected it like a huge shard of mirror.

"Who did this? What is it? Who is it?" Jenny asked in awe. The marble had been carved into the shape of a sitting figure. I'd been leaning against one of its folded legs.

"Nobody knows who made it," replied the professor. We gaped at the magnificent carving, so smooth against the rugged landscape. "Legend has it that this is the figure of the goddess of forests. She will protect the plants and animals below—but only if those who live on the mountain worship her and help protect it, too.

"Over a century ago, the palace at the top of this mountain was captured. By the British, to be precise. The capturers ridiculed the legend, and of course they didn't worship the goddess. Within decades, this forest, which had been pristine for centuries, had a railway line charging through it. It was opened up to hunters and ravaged of wildlife. Bulldozers came to cut down trees for hardwood. When the British eventually left, the palace was handed back to its rightful owners—my family." The professor paused, looking at his fingernails and deep in thought.

"My father wanted to restore the natural beauty of the landscape here. He knew the legend of the forest goddess. He took regular hikes to this carving to worship her. He stood up against the big logging companies and registered the forest as a protected area. But the companies would send their trucks in by night, and it's difficult to stop poachers. Stories spread about my father, about how he talked to animals and deities. He told newspaper reporters he could hear the bells of the goddess's anklet as she danced through the forest." He looked at us. "The papers reported that he'd gone mad."

I'd heard bells, too—when we'd seen the vultures. And other bells—in Greystanes, Angela's shop door, the opening of the paper mâché box. The forest magic had been with the tiger all along, I was sure of it… Either that, or I was going mad, too…

"My father was brave," continued the professor, "but he couldn't stand up to the logging firms and poaching rings on his own. He asked me to stay here with him and fight for the forest. I was young, foolish perhaps. I wanted to study in England, learn different ways of protecting our world, follow my own dreams…" His voice faltered. "Parents are funny beings," he muttered. "They teach you to think for yourself and then they want to tell you what to do."

The afternoon heat was heavy, and the feel of the mountain was changing. There was a battle going on here. The magic of the forest versus the outside world. Those who wanted to save this beautiful place from destruction, and those who only cared about how its riches might make them richer. There was even a battle between Menon and his father, though it sounded like they'd both been fighting for the forest in their own way. I thought of Baba and Naniji, always quarrelling. Now I realised the things they wanted were often the same.

"So, what does your father need to forgive you for?" Jenny asked the professor. "For going away?"

"Yes, correct," he sighed. "He said if I went to England, I was betraying him, betraying India. Memories of the Raj were bitter when he was growing up. It was British people that had disturbed the forest first, after all. He said if I went to England, he would banish me from our mountain home. He said I would no longer be his son."

"And you went anyway?" Jenny exclaimed.

"I went anyway," the professor replied, "and I didn't come back."

"But you wrote letters," Dilip said defensively.

"Yeah, but even then," Jenny wrinkled her nose, "he didn't come looking for you." The professor shook his head, not seeming to mind Jenny's total lack of tact.

"I felt so guilty about it all and the guilt began to overpower me," the professor's face looked pained. "I was scared I would never be forgiven. Every year I would send anonymous donations for the protection of the forest. It was my father's acceptance I wanted, really. I've been cowardly, and I cannot tell you how much it now means to me to be going back. I only hope it's not too late."

We didn't know what to say. A tiny greenfly landed on my wrist, where my watch used to be, then zipped off again.

"The sky's getting dark," I said, and we shifted up, gathering our things. I took the lead again, without being asked to this time. With each step, I tried to stamp out my growing worries. Slowly, painfully, we climbed to the top of the mountain.

22

REUNION

Towards the top, the jungle had reclaimed the thin path and we had to beat our way forwards through sharp grass and thorny branches. At last, we came to a road, flat and wide and leading to a tall gate. The professor clanged a cowbell at the side of the gate, and we peered through its braided metal bars into the grounds of what looked like a palace. A neat, lime lawn stretched to marble steps, which fanned up to the door of a magnificent white mansion. The professor clanged the bell a second time. There was no other sound. The sun was going down fast and there was a cold bite to the air. Just as the professor was reaching for the bell again, I saw someone in the dim light.

"Look!" I said, pointing to a man in gardening overalls carrying a Tilly lamp. He scurried across the lawn towards us, apologising over and over. When he reached us, he stopped abruptly and held his lamp up at the professor, faltering.

"Hello, Kam," said the professor. "Do you recognise me?"

There was a pause as the man swung his oil lantern across the rest of us. He rubbed his brow, a frown forming below the bandana he was wearing. He bowed to the professor and then unlocked the padlocks and untangled the chains. The gate swung open with a creak.

"These are my friends—Lal, Jenny, and Dilip. Kids, this is Kam. Kam and I used to play together when we were young. His father was the gatekeeper then, and I see that he is gatekeeper now," he bowed and laughed forwards, arms open to his old friend. "How good to see you, Kam!"

But Kam had stiffened up as if he didn't feel quite the same way as the professor about their reunion. Jenny, Dilip and I exchanged glances.

As we walked, the professor asked about stuff like the garden, the upkeep of the rooms, the other workers, and Kam answered boastfully, as though to say everything had been running just fine without him. But when Menon asked about his father, Kam's tone hardened.

"Prepare yourself, Menon," he said. "A great deal of time has gone by. He, like all of us, has aged. You will find your father an old man. After you left, he continued to work hard caring for the valley, but…" Kam hesitated.

"I shouldn't have left the way I did," Menon admitted.

"You… it nearly destroyed him."

I tripped over my own feet and Kam swung the lantern high to widen the circle of light. "What brings you back now?" he asked. "It's been so long." Kam's voice was tight with accusation.

"These children," the professor smiled at us. "They came with a message for me, sent a long time ago from my father. I have always believed he didn't want to see me again, but now I realise that maybe he did."

Kam's lip twisted unkindly towards us. Jenny looked at me sideways.

We walked on, the Tilly lamp squeaking as it swung. "Your father grieved for you a long time," he said. "He also grieved the loss of the tigers from his forest. The last one was shot shortly after you left."

"The *last* one?" Jenny cried.

"Sadly, Jenny, there are no tigers left in these parts," Menon said.

"No more tigers in this whole forest?"

"It's one of the reasons for my work with breeding programmes," Menon was sounding defensive. "Tiger species are highly endangered now. If we're not careful, we will lose them forever."

Jenny tried to ask more but we'd arrived at the entrance. All three of us kept close to the professor as we stepped into a dimly lit marble hall. Kam disappeared into a side door, returning with a butler, an old man wrinkly as a Medjool date. His eyes brimmed with tears when he saw the professor, and they hugged.

"Welcome back," he said. His voice was thin and weak. "Come in, come in, come this way. Your father is outside." The old butler took the professor's elbow. Kam stayed at the doorway as we were ushered forwards by the butler, and I was glad he wasn't joining us.

The butler drew back a sliding door leading to a large balcony with a white balustrade. Big pillars of jasmine grew on either side, and there was a hint of kerosene in the air from hanging lanterns. Night and its darkness had set in. A water fountain babbled somewhere in the black below.

Dilip was next to me, juddering, and I didn't know if the juddering was because the night was cold, or because (like me a bit) he was scared. I sidled closer to him. A shadow moved at the far end of the balcony. An old man was hunched there, looking out to the night. Menon moved towards him.

"Father," he said, in a broken sort of voice. The old man didn't turn around. The butler urged the professor forwards. "Father. It's me, Menon."

Still, the old man didn't move. The professor stepped forwards and touched him on the shoulder and the old man turned. His face in the lantern light was kind and sad. Suddenly, he gasped and collapsed into the professor's arms and they held each other tightly. I sort of wanted to look, but also wanted to look away, and was relieved when the old butler gestured for us to leave them and follow him back indoors.

In a great room, a fire was going. We took off our shoes and sat on a wicker mat and then the butler went away. I wondered where the tiger was, hoping it would be here soon. I didn't like the idea that it was the only one of its kind left in thousands of acres of forest. The butler came back, bringing with him a tray of hot bread rolls and warm, ginger-spiced orange juice. We didn't talk much as we gobbled our supper, but the professor and his father must have had a lot to say—they took ages.

Our eyes were closing over when they appeared. Even the butler was nodding off. Menon's father was properly old and frail—and for some reason I'd imagined he would have a beard and glasses like Menon, but he didn't have either. He swished his hands about when he spoke. He told us that every evening for nearly four decades he'd stood on the balcony and dreamed that Menon had called his name; he'd long ago stopped turning to find it was only his imagination.

"This time, though, it was real," he smiled, and pressed each of our foreheads firmly with his thumb, like a priest offering blessings. Jenny shrunk back a little and blushed.

"What about the tiger?" Dilip asked. "Is the tiger here yet?"

The old man told us that when he was out walking that afternoon, he'd seen a tiger. He'd assumed that his mind was, as usual, playing tricks on him. "But something tells me that this time it was real," he smiled.

"It must be real," Dilip yawned.

"And your yawning tells me it must be late," the old man said. "We can talk in the morning." He asked the butler to show us to our rooms.

Dilip and I shared a wide four-poster bed. The crisp sheets and soft pillow felt like a prize after our long trek. But as I lay awake listening to Dilip's breathing as he slept, I missed my own bed with its saggy mattress in the room with yellow walls. I'd lost count of how many nights we'd been away. I wondered what Mum and Baba were doing right now. Thoughts boiled over into dreams. Strange, fragmented dreams. Two men's voices danced round and round, in steps and pirouettes across the world's hallways. Naniji was singing. There was a *kraa, kraa* of a raven. A silver snake was slithering. The light from the gatekeeper's lantern flickered out.

23

I SPY

When we tiptoed down the flight of marble stairs the next morning, the butler was waiting for us. He took us to the breakfast room and poured us fruit juice. Jenny was still in bed.

I realised it was the place we'd crossed through the night before, where the sliding door opened out to the balcony. The butler opened the door. Cold morning air seeped in and sunlight dappled against the glass from a large overhanging tree I hadn't noticed in the black of night.

Menon came whistling in with his father and they sat down. The butler poured two cups of thick black coffee. Menon's father nodded at him, and then looked at us.

"Someone told me that you two boys are very good at I Spy. Is that true?"

"I am!" squeaked Dilip.

"Oh, good. Then here is one especially for you and

Lal," and the old man pressed the tips of his long fingers together. "I spy with my little eye, something beginning with T."

We scanned the room, and the old man shook his head at 'table', 'tiles', 'telephone', and 'teaspoon'—and then I saw it. I don't know how we'd not seen it before. There, sitting on the balcony, was the tiger. We scrambled up, hurling ourselves towards it. It curled around and around us, nearly knocking us over as it nuzzled against our shoulders. Its fur smelled of all our adventures and morning dew and, faintly, of Greystanes. Just then, Jenny arrived looking all groggy and grumpy—but as soon as she saw the tiger, she beamed and ran over.

Menon left—Kam had invited him to take breakfast with him in his quarters. We ate scrambled eggs on toast with Menon's dad, who turned out to be fun. He told us stories about Menon and gave us riddles to solve. He also told us about his anti-poaching work helping to educate local villagers, and how he and Kam had recently purchased a big cage so they could take injured animals to rescue centres. They had bought it with money sent from their anonymous donor, who turned out to have been Menon all these years! The tiger lay down in between me and Dilip, licking its coat, and I rested my feet against its warm back.

As the butler cleared the plates away. I looked around the big room. It was all so grand and, though not as different as Mani's gutter, still a million miles from the India I'd lived in.

After breakfast was cleared, Menon's father invited

us for a walk, to visit the place in the forest where he'd first met the tiger. Menon caught up with us as we left the garden at the back of the palace, following a path into the trees. His dad told us how he used to come this way to be alone after Menon had left. One day, when he reached a clearing, the tiger appeared out of the green and sat with him. The next time, and every time after that, the tiger joined him when he went for his walk in the forest. He began to talk to it, and then confide in it. "There is a deep magic here," he said, casting his eyes around.

"Of the forest goddess?" asked Jenny.

"Yes, perhaps," smiled the old man. "Dilip's feelings seem to have awakened it, too. Perhaps they were similar to mine. You missed your home; I missed my son."

I'd been homesick as well, I thought, wondering why the tiger hadn't chosen me. Even though I hadn't asked out loud, the old man sort of answered.

"You didn't just believe in the tiger, Dilip—you *trusted* it, the way I had before you." He bowed slightly to the tiger.

We walked in single file, Menon's father leading the way and walking quickly for someone so old. I was at the very back behind Menon. The tiger walked alongside us, half camouflaged in the bushes.

"So, what happened after you told the tiger your story?" Jenny asked.

"Ah, yes. Well, it promised to help me," he spoke to us over his shoulder. "As you know, tigers are excellent trackers. I thought it would be a good idea for me to give the tiger a message to carry to Menon—Menon's ring. His mother had given it to him; it was the one thing I knew would be a strong signal of how sorry I was and how much I wanted him to come home." I didn't reveal that his signal hadn't exactly been that clear when we'd first delivered it. "I told Kam about my plan and he agreed. We were powerless to do anything else."

He described the fateful day the tiger set off to track down Menon. He'd looped a small canvas purse, with the boxed ring inside it, around the tiger's neck, and watched as the tiger had padded away, its markings merging into the streaks of the jungle.

"I was on my way back home when I heard the gunshot," he stopped on the path. "I panicked. I ran back into the forest but lost my footing. Luckily, Kam arrived. He'd been on an anti-poaching patrol and heard the gunshot, too. There were so few people I could trust—poaching was at its peak—but I had Kam."

Menon greyed with guilt.

"Despite Kam's endless efforts to find the gunman, the poachers were never caught, and the tiger was never found." I went prickly all over. Someone had known where the tiger had ended up—was the man in the snake jacket connected to the poachers? The forest was becoming dense and the air sweet and earthy. It was sticky hot. We started to walk again.

"Kam has been good to you, Father," said Menon.

"Well, he searched for you, too—he went to England just after the tiger was shot, to try to find you. Believe it or not, he's just back from his latest attempt…" but the old man's words were fading ahead and I didn't hear what he was saying—Menon had stopped short just in front of me and was gasping for air and giddy.

"Are you OK?" I asked, but he clearly wasn't. He was bent down clutching his stomach. The others had rounded a corner on the thin, brown path; I could hear their footfalls and the old man's voice trailing away. "Dilip?" I called after them. "Jenny?" Menon was leaning, half kneeling, against a tree. "Help!"

Suddenly, the tiger appeared, emerging from thick ferns. It looked at me with its big, orange eyes and called out, loud and urgent. Soon, the others had joined us. Menon was gagging and vomiting foam into the bushes.

"What's happened?" Jenny cried. Menon's father rushed over. The professor was sweating and swaying and struggling to speak.

"Jenny, Dilip," the old man said, "run back the way we came—follow the path. Please, tell Kam to come quickly."

They sprinted away, and the old man and I pulled Menon to his feet. He was heavy and unsteady, but the tiger took his weight. He held on with quaking hands to the tufts at the back of its neck. Every few steps, we had to stop for Menon to crouch and retch. As the forest turned to lighter woodland, I saw the palace again through the trees. Menon's father was talking all the time in a reassuring tone, coaxing Menon to step forwards with the tiger.

As we climbed the last stretch to the garden, Dilip and Jenny appeared with the butler—they hadn't been able to find Kam. We helped Menon across to a patch of soft, shaded lawn and lowered him down. Panting and whimpering, he writhed on the grass. Froth gathered at the corners of his mouth and caught in his beard. His father propped up his head and wiped him clean with a handkerchief.

The butler pulled back his jacket sleeves and with gentle, ancient hands, checked Menon's eyes and pulse and prodded his stomach.

He looked up to us and with a thin but sure voice, said, "Poison."

24

THE SNAKE JACKET

On the count of three, we pulled Menon up into a sitting position. His father held his chin and forced open his clamped jaws so that the butler could insert a syringe, pushing a dark syrup to the back of Menon's throat. He swallowed and squirmed.

"Activated charcoal," the butler explained. He'd run to the house to get it. "He has expelled most of the poison, but this will stop him absorbing the rest." As he spoke, he rubbed in between Menon's shoulder blades.

"Will he be OK?" Jenny's voice trembled.

"Yes," the butler smiled. "He needs a doctor, but he should recover quickly. The dose was high but, as I said, he has got rid of most of it. Let's sit with him while this antidote sinks in."

My fists were tight.

"Who did this?"

Menon's father looked up. He had tears in his eyes.

"Perhaps this was a mistake."

"But, how could he be poisoned by mistake?"

The old man sighed. "Poison is an old, old poaching trick. Guns are too loud and trapped animals scream. Poison kills quietly. Poachers put it on bait. Perhaps there was a mistake…" but he sounded doubtful himself. The tiger was patrolling the garden around us, its tail flicking and ears twitching.

"I thought there weren't any tigers here anymore," said Jenny.

The old man was stroking Menon's forehead. "Perhaps someone tracked the tiger yesterday? But, you know, there are animals besides tigers that poachers kill and sell. Pangolins, antelope, snakes…" Menon began to writhe again, shaking his head before slumping back with his eyes closed. "Let's get him inside before the sun gets too high. We need extra hands—I wonder where Kam is?"

Since nobody knew Kam's whereabouts, we got the tiger to help lift Menon. It bent low enough for us to manoeuvre Menon on to its back, and it carried him lopsidedly across the lawn and into the marble palace.

The butler zipped ahead of us to open the curtains of a ground-floor room. He fetched a blanket. Menon lay down on a settee and his father pulled over a chair and sat with him.

The butler took us back to the place we'd waited the

night before. My stomach was twisting with worry, but at least the tiger was with us this time. It settled down on the mat. Jenny kept getting up to look out the window.

After a long time, the butler came in. He placed a tray of flatbreads and lemonade and a box on the table. "He's recovering well. The doctor cannot get here because the road is closed, but it is not an emergency. She has reassured us that we have done the right thing. Menon must rest but will be strong again after a good night's sleep. The rangers are coming by foot—they will be here soon to report on any sight of poachers." He opened the box and put it on the mat for us. It was filled with old photographs of Menon as a child. "I thought you might like to look through these."

"Look!" Jenny smiled at a snap of eleven-year-old Menon in a party hat. "Ooh, who's that?" she asked, pointing to a boy at the edge of the frame.

"Ah, that's Kam," replied the butler, and he shuffled out the room, taking the tiger with him to check on Menon. I picked up the photograph for a closer look. Sure enough, there was Kam, standing a little way off, watching Menon. There was something about his expression that made me uncomfortable. I riffled through the other pictures. Kam staring at Menon dressed up for his first day of school. Kam carrying Menon's suitcases. Kam saddling up Menon's pony. Kam, the servant on the side-lines. His expression was the same in all of the photographs. It was the expression he'd had when we'd first met him. I put the photos down, my mind whirring.

"I don't trust Kam," I said.

Jenny was sucking lemonade with her teeth on the edge of her glass. She burped—a habit she'd been developing since breakfast at Auntie's. "Well, he sure wasn't happy about Menon coming back, was he?" she said.

"No, and I don't think he's ever liked him much. Look at these," and I showed them the photographs. "What was Menon's dad saying about Kam going to England?" I hadn't heard it all properly—Menon had halted at that point in our walk.

"Oh, yeah," Dilip replied. "Kam searched for Menon in England, after the tiger was shot. Menon's dad sent him, to look for Menon."

"So, around the same time that Ecks would have been selling the rug?" I said.

Jenny gaped. "Angela said someone—a man from India—had been poking around, remember? If it was Kam, it means he knew what happened to the tiger after it was shot. He wanted the tiger and the message."

"And he's just come back from his latest visit," added Dilip.

"What?" I looked to Jenny.

"Dilip's right. Menon's dad said we wouldn't believe it, but Kam just came back yesterday from his latest trip to

London. He was looking for Menon but didn't find him. He said he got as far as tracing him to Mumbai but he wasn't in the hotel he was meant to be in."

Just then, my eye fell on another photograph. This one was taken at the gatehouse. It was a picture of Menon and Kam and, next to them, an older man—the gatekeeper—with his back to the camera. On his jacket, I could just make out the shape of a snake. My jaw dropped.

"Kam wasn't happy to see Menon," I said, "*Kam* was searching for Menon and the rug, *Kam* was at the conference looking for Menon."

"He even asked what hotel he was staying in!" Jenny clocked.

Dilip swallowed his mouthful and frowned. "Are you saying—?"

"That the man with the long hair and the snake jacket—it's Kam!"

"Oh no," Jenny's voice was quiet. "Kam invited Menon to have breakfast with him…"

Suddenly I remembered what Menon had said to me on the train—that if the snake-jacket man knew about the magic, he'd know the value of the tiger. Kam didn't just want rid of Menon, he wanted the magic, too. A magical tiger skin rug was priceless. Panic hissed up from my toes to my ears.

"The tiger," I heard myself saying. "Where's the tiger?"

Jenny had paced back to the window. "Oh, no. Oh, no,

no, no..." She threw herself round—Dilip was already running. We all ran as fast as we could, into the great hallway, out onto the steps, down and across the lawn to where the tiger stood, facing Kam.

25

CAGED

To the side of the gatehouse was a big metal cage, the kind you'd get in olden-day circuses—I knew it must be the one Menon's father had spoken about at breakfast. Its door was wide open. Between Kam and the cage, the tiger stood, statue-still. Kam had a long, home-made looking whip in one hand, and as we got near, he thrashed it against the turf on either side of the tiger. We slowed down, panting. They both stood firm and focused.

Kam turned briefly, breaking his stare to gauge us. He was chewing paan—Naniji hated paan—a betel leaf and special nut that oozed red liquid. Kam spat some out onto the grass.

"Get back," he ordered and cracked the whip again, inching forwards, forcing the tiger backwards and closer to the cage.

"It was *you*, wasn't it?" I demanded. "*You* poisoned Menon, and now you want to steal the tiger. You failed to get the tiger rug from Greystanes, but you knew the magic was still there and now the tiger is here, you think you can get it."

Kam sneered, tensing his arms outwards as he concentrated on keeping the tiger in its place. The tiger's stillness was disconcerting.

Jenny took a brave step forward. "You didn't want Menon to come back, so you've been stopping him all these years. You never really looked for him in England—you just wanted the message back, in case he got it." Kam spat again and moved to the left slightly as the tiger dipped its head low and crouched down, one paw edging forwards.

I had a flashback to Ecks Auctioneers, to the butterfly on the paper-mâché box. Kam had discovered from Joseph Ecks that the magic was still alive, when the box didn't open. But how had he known where to go?

"You knew the poachers," I realised out loud. "You found out from the poachers where the tiger skin rug had been sent."

But it was clear that Kam was not going to tell us anything. He was moving forwards again, but the tiger gave a low growl, its eyes fixed on its opponent. Kam's hand on the whip handle was quivering.

He untied his bandana and his dark hair fell to his shoulders. As it did, a horrible fear set in. We were in Kam's way, and he didn't like things getting in his way.

He never had. Kam had wanted all along to get rid of Menon, and he'd go to any lengths to achieve it—even poison. My heart was beating so fast, but I wanted him to know his plans wouldn't work. My words came out choked. "Menon didn't die," I said. "Your plans aren't working. The tiger won't go with you—you can't command it. You have to stop now."

Down came the whip again and Kam yelled out and snarled. This time, the tiger snarled back. It pounced towards Kam, paws launching forwards, claws curled out. But Kam was quick, and darted out of its way, bringing the whip down against the tiger's back. The tiger twisted and growled in fury.

Jenny pulled us all away from the gatehouse as Kam and the tiger sidestepped around in a circle, Kam still trying to force the tiger back towards the metal cage behind. The tiger's ears were pulled tight back, its jaws open a crack. Kam drew in the long leather strap and then cast it low to the ground, whipping at the tiger's shins. All of a sudden, its low puckering growl became a roar. The roar was so loud and strong it shook the air. And as it roared, the tiger pounced towards Kam and over him, beating down to the ground at Kam's back. Turning to face the tiger, Kam tried again to trip it with his whip, but every time he lashed out, the tiger bounded and appeared behind or to the side of him.

Jenny pulled us back further, until we were flat up

against the wrought-iron gates and would be cornered if Kam should turn on us. But the tiger wasn't going to let that happen. It drew up on its hind legs, thrusting its bodyweight forwards to bear down with open jaws towards Kam. Kam's arm flew out with the whip, but this time the tiger caught the whip-handle with its teeth, biting it from Kam's grip. Kam gasped and froze, defenceless without his weapon. There was nothing he could do, nowhere he could run. Sinking low to the ground, hackles up, the tiger steered Kam backwards, his arms up in surrender, into his own trap. We didn't falter—the three of us ran to close the metal cage doors, padlocking Kam inside.

The tiger huffed and prowled around the cage. It seemed truly wild, and its wildness meant not even Dilip dared go closer, let alone launch in for a hug. A voice called out and the tiger retreated, vanishing into the trees behind the gatehouse.

From the far side of the palace, some figures appeared—the butler and three rangers. And at one of the palace windows, I glimpsed another figure—Menon's father. He stood and nodded down at me and I wondered how much he had seen.

The rangers arrested Kam based on our jumbled-up account and the butler's insistence that we were telling the truth. We watched in dumbfounded silence as they took him away in handcuffs, to a far room in the palace for questioning. The butler led us back to Menon and his father to face an interrogation of our own.

Menon was lying back on the settee, wrapped in blankets and sipping water. We told them everything, all about the snake jacket and the photos and the butterfly box, all in a mixed-up order. Menon's father looked completely exhausted, all the fun of the morning's riddles and rhymes gone.

"So, Kam knew who the poachers were," he said in a sad voice. "And he let them get away with it. Often there is a weak link in anti-poaching, someone on the inside who sees an opportunity to make some money."

"The double-crossing—" Jenny started, but then bit her tongue as if to stop bad words flying out.

"Perhaps I didn't do enough to reassure him he'd always have a place here," the old man said, wringing his hands. But the butler shook his head.

"No, it isn't that. You've always been generous. Kam had much more than most, but even as a child he was never happy with what he had, always wanting more."

"But did he really poison Menon?" Dilip still needed to know. We looked over to where Menon lay sweating and shivering. Just at that moment, one of the rangers knocked on the door and stepped in.

"Kam is not talking much sense," the ranger reported,

"but he has confessed his wrongdoing. I think we should take him to the police station at first light. He's muttering about magic and tigers and something about burning letters that Menon sent… He seems confused. I think he's in shock."

We were all in shock. There was so much to take in. The butler suggested we all have something to eat and then go for an early night. Before we did, he went down to the gatehouse to invite the tiger out of the forest and out of hiding.

26

HOME TIME

Early the next morning after the rangers and Kam had gone, we gathered at the front of the palace. The tiger crouched low so that Jenny, Dilip and I could climb onto its back. Menon's father stepped forwards and touched the tiger's mane, speaking to it in their magic way.

Just as the doctor had said, Menon's strength had returned after a solid night of sleep. As we sat high on the tiger's back, he beamed at each of us in turn. "Thank you, Dilip," he said, "for believing in the tiger. Jenny, thank you for believing in your friends. And Lal," he clapped his hand to my shoulder, "you are a true leader—thank you for believing in yourself."

I couldn't speak to say any of the things I wanted to say and when I blinked, hot tears rolled down my cheeks, drying in itchy. I wiped them with my jacket sleeve.

"Will we see you again?" Jenny's cheeks were burning, too.

"I can't see why not," the professor smiled. "Perhaps I could write to Mr. and Mrs. Patel, tell them I've heard about their tiger skin rug, ask if I can take a look…"

"Oh yes, please!" Jenny nodded and we all agreed. Menon patted the tiger's hind and stepped backwards.

The tiger rolled its shoulders lightly, swaying on its paws and bending its legs as it prepared to pounce. I put my arms around Dilip's waist. The tiger pressed down and then sprung up and into the sky. With the fluttering in my tummy and buzzing in my head, it took a few moments for me to look down. The tiger tipped to its side in the air, its front paws forward. There below, on the lime green lawn, Menon, his father and the old butler were watching and waving, craning their necks upwards.

We flew over emerald hills and brown flatlands and out to the sparkling ocean. The tiger was taking us westwards, away from the sun, against time and into the night. It stretched out below us and we huddled, like we had on our first flight, into the middle of the rug, fighting surges of cold air and tiredness. The remaining sun-touched clouds were soon gone, replaced by stars dotting the sky. The tiger glowed a ghostly amber and sparks trailed from its edges in the dark.

I stirred and looked around—wooden floorboards, an upright piano, green-painted walls. Greystanes. The tiger's skin was flat and rough. It seemed more lifeless than ever before. Sitting up at the torn tail-end, I tucked in a thread coming loose where the skin had been stitched to the backing cloth. Dead tiger skin. My heart skipped as I shook Dilip and Jenny awake. Dilip stretched and yawned, his eyes still full of dreams.

"We're back," Jenny murmured and bit her lip—we knew what this meant. As we pulled ourselves up, Dilip edged around to the tiger's face. He lowered his chin and I thought he might cry, but instead of crying, he whispered.

This time, as the tiger took shape, the rug itself remained on the floor. The spirit of the big cat, wavering like a hologram, drew itself up to a standing position. Dilip placed his hands gently on its cheeks and they touched noses until Dilip let go of the tiger's face to cover his own. Jenny squeezed around its neck.

"I won't forget you," she said, her voice trembling.

And then it was my turn.

I held up my hand. The tiger leaned its forehead against my palm, and its magic—that strange electricity —tingled through me. But I didn't want its magic now; I wanted the warmth of its fur, real and whole. As I hugged it close, I couldn't keep in my tears. Why did we have to say goodbye?

A gust of air blew in from the glass doors. The tiger turned its head to the change in light, the pale glints of morning. It lifted a paw and after only a moment's hesitation, stepped off the rug. We followed it out and across the grass, stopping at the entrance to the Hidden Garden to let the tiger pad alone to the middle of the stones—it wasn't taking us with it on this journey.

It blinked slowly. And I heard it, at last—its language —its voice. 'Thank you', the tiger said. And then it turned from us and circled the air with its pink nose. Without looking back, it hunched its shoulders, and, bounding upwards, vanished into the morning sky.

In the silence that followed, I realised I'd been holding my breath, and also holding one of Dilip's hands. Jenny had his other hand. We stood like that for a while, a feeling of peace settling over the garden. We hadn't been ready for the tiger to leave, but it had been waiting for such a long time to go.

"Lal?" Mum's voice came from the verandah, where she stood hugging into her peach towelling dressing gown. "Lal, Dilip? And Jenny?" Dilip and I scrambled across the grass and threw our arms around her. So much had happened. I'd missed her so much. Mum pinched my chin up between her finger and thumb and smiled. "What's the matter? What are you doing outside, and so early?"

We waited for her to tell us how angry and disappointed she was at our running away, how sick with worry she'd been—but she wasn't in the slightest bit any of those things. She was being normal, bustling back indoors and across to the hearth, Dilip still wrapped around her, to light a morning fire.

Lighting a fire. She only ever did that on Saturdays, and it was on Friday night that we'd left—had we been away a whole week?

"Time I got the kettle on, I think," said Mum, glancing to the mantel-top. "Oh, this ancient old thing has stopped again!" She reached for the clock, and as she turned it to fix its pendulum, I saw its hands, unmoving at eleven o'clock. Eleven o'clock—the exact time it had been when we'd set off with the tiger!

Time had taken care of itself.

"What's the actual time, Lal?" Mum looked to the pale strip on my wrist where my watch used to be.

"I… I lost my watch," I said.

"Oh, Lal, how? Where?" she asked and, when I didn't answer straight away, she sighed. "Never mind, we'll discuss that later." And as she left the Drawing Room, she called over her shoulder, "Jenny, come back for lunch—and bring your Granny!"

Naniji had decorated the dining room with freshly picked flowers, gathered in bright bunches. The table was decked with dishes of steaming rice and fragrant curries, little bowls of fried chilli peppers and spicy kale. Mr. Stirling arrived, followed by Jenny and Granny. Everyone was talking over everyone else and laughing across each other as we ate. Baba wanted to talk to me about his *Hindu's Who's Who of Who's Here*. Mum asked Mr. Stirling for advice and Naniji gave Mr. Stirling advice he hadn't asked for. He was delighted to be here, he said—Miss Will hadn't invited anyone in after she'd become unwell.

"What was the matter with her?" Dilip enquired.

"Dementia." He shook his head. "She was hearing and seeing things—at one point she even imagined there were bells in the roof and a real tiger living in Greystanes!"

Jenny nearly choked on her chapatti.

After we ate, Mum sent us to the verandah, insisting that a brew of "good Scottish tea" would pep us up. Granny read our fortunes in our tea leaves. The afternoon light was dramatic; even though the sky was deep grey, the entire lawn was lit in a warm, golden glow. It was such a relief to be home.

This was home, then, after all. The tiger had kept its promise to the old man on the mountain, but it hadn't forgotten its promise to us. When Dilip had asked the tiger to take us home, we'd thought home was India. But India hadn't felt like home at all. Not in the gutter, not at the palace. Not without Ajay or our old house or Mum and Baba. The tiger must have known that home doesn't have to be just one place, or any place at all.

I thought about everything that had happened. The Customer Services Manager at Waterloo hadn't thought we belonged because we looked like runaways. For the postie in the alleyway, our home was a fixed address where a stamped letter could be sent. Home for Angela was somewhere she'd never even been; and Mani lived in a drainpipe—her home was her street gang and a kind, adopting Auntie.

For me, home was sitting right here. It was Mum's soft smile, Baba's big ideas, Naniji's scented saris and Granny's pancakes. Home was sitting on the verandah in the late afternoon sun or being inside grey stone walls when it drizzled.

The tiger had taken us to India, but it had brought us home.

THE END

ACKNOWLEDGEMENTS

Many thanks to my publisher and editor, Anne Glennie, for her kindness and commitment. Thanks to Kelly Macdonald for her work promoting my book and to the booksellers and librarians who place it on (and readers who take it off) their shelves. I am very grateful to my sister, Marian Brown, for her advice and gorgeous illustrations, Darren Gate for his technical help, and Tanny Gill for checking my Hindi. I am lucky to have had the support of Melvin Burgess, 'Clan Cranachan', Tricia Lancaster, Joan Lennon, the Moniack Mhor class of 2015, and my writing and editing buddy, Miranda Moore.

In the creation of this book, I am indebted (in all sorts of ways) to friends and family, with special nods to the Brown, James, Moore and Schmoll families, Kim Crosbie, Auntie Irene, Auntie Sandra and Uncle Jim, my fabulous parents and sisters, and my cats. And, of course, to Lawrence, Andrew and Adrian. Thank you for believing in me.

Tigers (*Panthera tigris*) are the biggest of the wild cats. After a century of deforestation, habitat destruction, hunting and poaching, there are now fewer than 4,000 left in the wild.

I would like to acknowledge those who are working to save them and the ecosystems they thrive in, because when tigers and other species become extinct, no amount of magic can bring them back to life.

ABOUT THE AUTHOR

Joan Haig, born in Zambia, was weaned on avocados and stories. When she was twelve, her family moved to the happy isles of Vanuatu in the South West Pacific. She has lived, worked and travelled all over the world, most recently settling with her husband, children and cats into a little cottage in the Scottish Borders.

She currently works in Edinburgh for Arcadia University's College of Global Studies.

Her writing dream is that her stories are enjoyed by children across Scotland and beyond—and touch some grown-up hearts along the way.

www.joanhaigbooks.com
Instagram @joanhaigbooks